Flame in Snow

SERAFIM OF SAROV
A conventionalised contemporary portrait
Artist unknown

Flame in the Snow

A life of St. Serafim of Sarov

Julia de Beausobre

TEMPLEGATE PUBLISHERS

Text © 1996 Constance Babington Smith

Introduction © 1996 Donald Nicholl

Templegate Publishers
302 East Adams Street
Springfield, IL 62701

ISBN 0-87243-223-8

Without limiting the rights under copyright reserved above, no part of this publication may be reproduced, stored in or introduced into a retrieval system, or transmitted, in any form, or by any means (electronic, mechanical, photocopying, recording, or otherwise), without the prior written permission of the above publisher of this book.

Introduction

It was baking hot in the heartland of Russia during the month of July, 1903, as hundreds of thousands of Russians from all corners of the land made their way on foot and on horseback, by boat and by carriage and even by home-made carts towards the vast monastic complex of Sarov, situated in the province of Tambov, about one hundred miles from the great trading centre of Nizhny-Novgorod on the river Volga. The pilgrims were drawn from every rank in Russian society, from high-ranking generals to homeless beggars; and the crowds jostling along the dusty roads included a bewildering variety of ethnic groups, some of whom had been tramping for months. They were all drawn towards Sarov to witness and celebrate the canonization of the monastery's most famous *starets*, Serafim, on the anniversary of his birthday, the 19th of July.

The crowds had already been gathering for weeks in the fields around the monastery which had been turned into one huge encampment. Sheds and tents had been erected to receive the pilgrims; shops and stalls were set up so that everyone might be fed; and from morning until nightfall the sun shone down upon them as the faithful attended endless acts of devotion extending even into the depths of the moonlit nights. Their excitement mounted when the Tsar Nicholas II and the Tsaritsa Aleksandra, accompanied by their family and bands of courtiers, arrived on the 17th of July. The liturgy of canonization itself, in the presence of Serafim's relics, lasted from five in the afternoon until ten at night. "It was so beautiful," writes one eye-witness, "that in spite of the fierce July heat, no one asked 'When will it end?'"

Throughout the whole celebration the warmth and devotion of the people for the Tsar and his family was felt by all. But that was the last occasion on which the nation of Russia was to be at ease with itself before the storms of revolution broke over the land.

Amongst the earliest victims of those storms were the monks of Sarov and the Sisters of the neighbouring convent of Diveyevo, whom the Bolsheviks scattered throughout the Russian land in March, 1927. At the same time the precious relics of Serafim were carried off to Moscow. There they were put on display in the Museum of Godlessness as an exhibition of unmasked superstition. Soon it seemed to many observers, both in Russia and throughout the rest of the world, that everything Serafim stood for was nothing more than a relic of a world that was dead and gone for ever.

True, there were one or two living relics who still clung to that seemingly dead world, as was illustrated by an incident that took place about the year 1930 in the Museum of Godlessness. It was on July 19, the birthday of St. Serafim, when the attendant in the room where his relics were displayed, herself a secret believer, noticed an old peasant standing hesitantly in the doorway. He was holding branches of pine and fir in his hands. Thinking that the man must have lost his way the woman asked him what he was looking for. He replied, "It's this way, *matouchka*. They have taken away our *batiouchka* Serafim, and I have heard that he is here now. I come from Sarov and I thought it would please him if I brought him a bit of something from the forest. He loved the forest so much." So the attendant pointed to the saint's casket and the peasant knelt and laid his branches there.

The following year the peasant came again on Serafim's birthday, once more bringing branches. But that was the last time. It was not the last time for Serafim, however, (in spite of the fact that during the dark night of the Russian soul even his very relics were lost). Because in December 1990 the Museum of Atheism in Leningrad was undergoing a radical reorganization in the course of which a group of the museum staff came across some old packing cases in a long-neglected storeroom, and when they opened one of them they discovered a skeleton around the neck of which was a copper cross. It proved to be the same cross that Serafim's mother had placed around the neck of her beloved son as he was setting out on foot, in November 1778, to become a monk at Sarov. The relics of St. Serafim, long believed to have been irretrievably lost, had been found!

That discovery gave birth to an eruption of joy throughout the whole of Russia. Liturgies of thanksgiving continued to be offered in hundreds of churches, and for almost six months the relics became a focus of devotion in the Patriarchal Cathedral of the Epiphany in Moscow. Then from July 23, 1991, until August 1, they were borne in procession from

Moscow by road across the Russian heartland by way of Bogorodsk, Vladimir and Nizhny-Novgorod, to the recently reestablished convent of Diveyevo, where they now rest. The procession was greeted by millions of people as it passed through towns and villages. Indeed, as it moved out of Nizhny-Novgorod the throngs who came to honour it were lined up for a distance of nine miles.

The reason why Serafim's reliquary had to be taken to the convent at Diveyevo rather than to Sarov was because the little town of Sarov had ceased to exist in 1940 and had become the centre of Arzamas-16, a secret, closed military zone. Entrance to the whole area has ever since been severely restricted because it was here that Andre Sakharov and his scientific colleagues developed the Soviet Union's hydrogen bomb and cruise missiles. This contraposition of Serafim's relics and the nuclear bomb holds apocalyptic significance for many Russians, one of whom has written, "The enemy of the human race must have taken a heavy toll if, even where St. Serafim preached Eternal Life in the Resurrected Lord, not only have godless deeds been carried out, but a cult of death in its most advanced technocratic manifestation has ruled supreme...."

What manner of man, then, was this Serafim who continues, irrepressibly, to serve as the light in the darkness of our world? The chief authority on Russian spirituality, George Fedotov, has written, "in Serafim we are presented with a personality of extraordinary spiritual endowments, with gifts of a higher order than can be tested by the religious historian with purely rational methods."

Little is known in detail about the years previous to his

becoming a monk. He was born in 1758 and given the name Prokhor at baptism. His family were well-respected as brick-makers and builders in his native city of Kursk, a city whose population of 8,000 souls were noted throughout Russia for their skill as merchants and traders. Isidore Mashnin, his father, had been entrusted in 1752 with the enterprise of building a great church there, to be dedicated to St. Sergius and the Kazan icon of the Mother of God, based upon a plan designed by the famous architect Bartholomew Rastrelli. Sadly Isidore himself died in 1760; but his wife Agatha, a splendid woman revered by all, took upon herself the task of overseeing the construction and was rewarded by seeing it consecrated many years later.

It was whilst Agatha was superintending the work on the bell-tower one day, with the seven-year old Prokhor alongside her, that he fell from the height of the tower. Yet, miraculously, in the eyes of witnesses, he suffered no harm. It was enough to lead the local fool for Christ to remark that it showed Prokhor to be "one of God's elect." The young boy himself attributed his preservation to the protection of Mary the Mother of God, an explanation he was also to give on many other occasions throughout the rest of his life when he was miraculously cured of serious illnesses. Indeed, there are so many similar instances described by Serafim that anyone who denies their possibility is calling into question the witness of Serafim himself, as well as discounting the possibility that we are, in the words of the Epistle to the Hebrews, "encompassed about by a great cloud of witnesses," a truth to which Serafim's own life is itself such a powerful witness.

During the next few years Prokhor grew in piety but delayed his entry into Sarov until the life work of the Mashnin family was consummated on October 22, 1788, the day that the Kazan Church of the ikon of the Mother of God was consecrated.

By virtue of the work of various scholars, Prokhor's life, once he became the monk Serafim, is easier to summarize with confidence than was possible when Julia de Beausobre was composing *Flame in the Snow*. To begin with, we have a reliable description of his appearance. He was five feet ten inches tall, broad shouldered and strongly built. His hair was thick and light brown, as were his bushy eyebrows, though both hair and eyebrows were to turn white in later life. His nose was finely shaped and people used to remark how deep his voice was when he spoke. But what commanded attention above all were his strikingly light blue eyes.

Certain dates which can be worked out from the written sources marking the stages of his monastic journey, may help the reader to keep track of Julia de Beausobre's narrative. They are here listed in summary fashion as below:

From November 20, 1778 until August 13, 1786, his status was that of a novice under the guidance of a wise old monk, Father Joseph. For three of those years he was ill with dropsy, much of the time confined to his bed. He was cured through a vision of the Mother of God, about which he himself said, "there appeared to me the Most Holy Mother of God with the Apostle John the Theologian. Pointing towards me the Sovereign Lady said, 'Here is one of us!'"

Soon afterwards he accompanied Fr. Joseph on foot, begging alms for the monastery. The two of them visited

Kursk where they were overjoyed to discover his mother still living.

Having made his solemn profession and taken the name Serafim on August 8, 1786, he was ordained a deacon two months later.

The year 1788 saw the foundation in the neighbouring village of Diveyevo of a community of devout women — though they were not canonically nuns. On June 13 of the following year the foundress died, but not before she had exacted a promise from the Abbot of Sarov, Pakhomius, and his young companion Serafim, that they would take care of her little community.

Serafim was ordained a priest on September 2, 1793, but the next year his beloved superior, Pakhomius, died, to be succeeded as abbot by another confidant of Serafim's, Isaiah. It was Isaiah who secured permission for him to become a hermit and inhabit a small hut in the forest some three and one-half miles distant from the monastery. He went there on November 21, 1794, exactly sixteen years to the day since he entered the monastery. There followed the thousand days and nights of his unceasing prayer.

This period of his eremitical life was brought to a violent end on September 12, 1804, when he was gravely wounded by robbers. Once more his life was saved through the Mother of God. But from now on, for the rest of his life, he was bent and in pain, and he needed the aid of a stick or an axe to support him whilst walking. His hair had turned completely white.

In the year 1806 Father Isaiah resigned his office and Serafim, who by this time was serving as *starets* for many of the monks, was elected to succeed him but declined. In his stead the treasurer, Niphont, took over the monastery and gave it a very different direction. Serafim ceased to act as *starets* but began the spiritual direction of the Sisters at Diveyevo.

After the death of Father Isaiah (December 4, 1807) Serafim, so as not to be a source of discord in the monastery, went to occupy the nearer hermitage in the forest, slightly more than a mile from the community. He spent three years in total silence and isolation. But in August, 1810, Niphont and the monastic council insisted that he must return to live in the monastery and attend the Sunday eucharist. Serafim obeyed but remained in silence, establishing himself as a recluse in one of the cells. By this time crowds of visitors were coming to Sarov simply to see Serafim in procession from his cell to the monastic church and back, in silence. Finally he put an end to his seclusion in 1813.

From then on he began to receive visitors and to guide the community of Sisters at Diveyevo, even deciding administrative and material affairs for them as if knowing that his message was to be handed on by Diveyevo rather than by Sarov. In consequence Bishop Jonas of Tambov was called in by Niphont to examine Serafim because of rumours about his relations with the Sisters (1821). Jonas declared the rumours to be false. The following year witnessed the first of his healing "miracles." The beneficiary of that healing, Michael Manturov, was to become a "pillar" of Diveyevo.

On November 25, 1825, he resumed his life in the hermitage when more and more people flocked to him. That same year the young priest of Diveyevo, Fr. Basil, was appointed by Serafim as the second "pillar" of the Sisters. During the succeeding two or three years, under Serafim's direction from a distance, a working mill was set up to enable a group of the Diveyevo sisters to be independent enough to lead a special form of communal life. And not long afterwards the third "pillar" for the support and protection after Serafim's death of the Diveyevo community was established in the person of Nicholas Motovilov, a highly intelligent young man from a land-owning family in the provinces of Simbirsk and Nizhny-Novgorod.

Motovilov was the beneficiary of another of Serafim's healings on September 5th, 1831, and later he was the interlocutor in Serafim's celebrated *Conversation on the Holy Spirit* which took place in November, 1831.

The year 1832 saw suspicion once more being cast upon Serafim's relations with the Sisters of Diveyevo, as a result of which in August Bishop Arsenius of Tambov came to examine Serafim. He left, like Bishop Jonas before him, not only convinced of Serafim's innocence but also of his sanctity. Serafim died on January 2, 1833.

Why, therefore, since the written records yield reliable dates of accounts of events and names of characters, do we need to read Julia de Beausobre's work *Flame in the Snow?* For her book, as she herself tells us in her Preface, is based upon the floating popular legends she heard during the period which she spent in the labour camp and described in her book *The Woman Who Could Not Die*.

One answer is that in order to come closer to Serafim we have to enter imaginatively into his world, into the very physical atmosphere of the forest, into the peculiar demands of the climate in that part of Tambov province, the mental habits, the superstitions of the people and the yearly round of Russian Orthodox piety. And through having lived in the midst of all these aspects of Russian life and traditions Julia de Beausobre manages to stimulate our imaginations, to say nothing of how she evokes for us the impact on that world of wider events in Russia and beyond.

Even more important, in view of George Fedotov's statement that Serafim enjoyed "extraordinary spiritual endowments, with gifts of a higher order than can be tested by the religious historian with purely rational methods," is that Julia de Beausobre, though in minor measure, was herself similarly gifted. Numerous reliable witnesses have testified to the fact that especially towards the end of her life she became almost transparent, as though for her the veil between this world and another world was getting ever thinner — as it was for Serafim whose example she followed in her unceasing intercession for the suffering. When one visitor at this time asked her how she spent her time she replied, "Scouring the face of the earth, using the carnal remnants of my decomposing body as a rag in God's hands to cleanse the world of its many pollutions." Such ascetic discipline enabled her to enter into the world of the Spirit inhabited by Serafim and so transmit to us truths about him which reason alone could not have attained.

Consider, for example, the following paragraphs to which I have returned time and again over the course of the past half-century and which may well serve as a meditation for anyone preparing to read the book itself:

Men have two ways of communicating with each

other: they speak, and perceive the pattern of human thought, they look into each other's faces, and gain vision of human life; neither can be acquired second hand.

In communicating through speech, words are our instrument: an instrument, potentially, of great precision. Entering deeper into the realm of silence, Serafim completely stemmed the flow of words within him. Not only the flow of spoken words; even the flow of words that well up in the mind. He joined the host which supplicates, lauds, and blesses without words.

His mute exchange of friendliness with the beasts raised their mutual understanding to a new rung of perfection. His prayer ceased to be a logical sequence of words. The name of Jesus, the essence of the constant prayer, ceased to be a word; it became the direction of his soul in its flight Godward; the tone of his soaring soul.

The tone was Jesus. And the direction was Jesus. Tone and direction blended. The velocity, received from the initial impetus, heightened. When it reached the limits of the notion of speech, he entered a realm more perfectly still than any other. In this realm, his mind was trained to hear the primordial word.

When the ebb set in, and human life was once more spread out before his mind's eye as a concrete network of ordinary facts, the fabric of particular human lives appeared before him with its particular design; the pattern that every one of these lives should follow was obvious to him. Men's mistakes — intentional and unintentional, in the present, past, and future — stood out as clearly discernible blotches and tangles. They disfigured the particular pattern of divine purpose. (pp. 107-108)

Finally, may I be permitted, in the space of two or three paragraphs, to suggest for the reader's consideration some features of Serafim's life which are specially significant for our own day.

Let me begin with the question my students often put to me, which was, "What is so special for you about this man? After all, he spent all those years in the forest on his own when he could have been doing something useful such as helping to educate the people or working to put an end to serfdom." The answer I invariably gave ran something like this: "All my life I have been fascinated by those people who are capable of doing wonderful and difficult things as if it were no effort. They perform such feats gracefully — great violinists, for instance, or ballet dancers or footballers. In the case of Serafim his instrument was his life. Hence, when he came out of the forest his every word, his every gesture, his very presence was healing to all the people around him. Grace had become his second nature.

"And in order to realize the uniqueness of that achievement perhaps we should ask ourselves a personal question: 'Out of all the millions of words that I have spoken in the course of my life, have I ever managed to speak one — even one, truly healing word to another human being?' — pleasant words, yes; kind words, yes; true words, yes.....But healing words?"

The sphere in which the need for such healing is most obvious, and where the touch of Serafim can be vital, was highlighted by Thomas Merton, who was deeply devoted to Serafim, when he wrote, "If I can unite in myself the thought and devotion of Eastern and Western Christendom, the Greek and Latin Fathers, the Russians with the Spanish mystics, I can prepare in myself the reunion of divided Christians."* And Merton is not the only one to have seen the remarkable affinity between Serafim and St. Francis of Assisi as a source of such reunion. For who, after studying the lives of these two great saints, one of the West and one of the East, could fail to associate Francis' affection for the wolf of Gubbio with Serafim's for the bear of Sarov? Or could fail to hear the same note of joy in the first's praise for sun and moon and water and the second's love of the trees and herbs and the winds of the forest? Both of them spent most of their days and nights in the open air. Together they are the universal saints of the environment.

There is one other wound that has afflicted the human family into which these two great saints can pour their healing balm. I am referring to the fractured relationship between the men of the family and the women of the family which has perhaps been made worse in our day through certain attempts to heal the fracture. Francis and Serafim have shown us the only way to do that — by their free and unclouded relationships with the women they loved and who loved them. In the case of Francis, for example, one thinks

Confessions of a Guilty Bystander p. 12.

not only of St. Clare but also of the noble Roman woman who came to him when he was dying, bringing him the marzipan cakes which he liked so much. Some of the friars did not want to let a woman into the enclosure but Francis himself pronounced her to be a friar for the present purpose. In the case of Serafim one remembers the Sister who was nervous about descending from the hayrick and whom Serafim took into his arms to lift her down. When Niphont looked askance at such behaviour Serafim told him that it was a great fault to be scandalized. Serafim and Francis had each entered into the freedom of the children of God, way beyond scandal.

Donald Nicholl

BIBLIOGRAPHY

St. Seraphim of Sarov. Valentine Zander SPCK 1975.
Seraphim de Sarov. Irina Gorainoff. Abbaye de Bellefontaine. 1976.
Saint Seraphim. Sarov et Diveyevo. Etudes et Documents. Vsevolod Rochcau. Abbaye de Bellefontaine. 1987.
Prepodobnyi Seraphim Sarovskii. Monastyr sv. Iova Pochaevskovo Munich-Moscow. 1993.
Letopis Seraphimo — Diveyevskavo Monastir. ed. L. Tchitgchagov 1903. Reprinted. St. Hermann of Alaska Monastery. 1978.

CONTENTS

FOREWORD .. .. p. 7

PART ONE—GODWARD BOUND

THE CALL .. .. p. 15

THE WAY .. .. p. 33

THE PLACE .. .. p. 54

THE FIGHT .. .. p. 77

PART TWO—RETURN MANWARD

THE SILENCE .. .. p. 101

THE OTHER FACE .. .. p. 109

THE SIMPLE SOUL .. .. p. 129

THE CONSUMMATE BIRTH .. .. .. p. 151

NOTE ON BIOGRAPHICAL DATA .. .. .. p. 163

FOREWORD

About ten years ago, I was nursing the sick in a Russian lumber camp south-east of Moscow. A snug yet roomy fifty-year-old house, built by a former owner of the forest for his agent, was placed at the disposal of our hospital. It was of wood and brick, had ample tiled stoves, double windows, two large balconies—one facing east the other west—and was surrounded by a sturdy brood of squat outhouses. Beyond the fence, the forest stretched for miles, murmuring with birch leaf and pine needle in summer, crackling with frost in winter. Our hospital served about a third of the huge, widely dispersed camp in which malaria was general, gastric and kidney complaints usual, epidemics and professional accidents frequent. Access to the hospital was least difficult along a narrow wedge of somewhat thinner forest where bumpy winding roads fanned out to " the villages." Intercourse between villagers and personnel was frowned upon at Camp Headquarters; but our transport and provisioning often broke down, while a peasant's sledge with eggs and milk, or home-churned butter and home-made cheese, slips easily along the winter snow-track; and in summer everyone in the neighbourhood goes berrying and mushroom-gathering with deep, funnel-like baskets made of birch-bark. Moreover, in a hospital of many deaths, a little medicine can often be spared for an out-patient in grave need; and a warm-hearted practitioner with a keen conscience does not like to refuse his professional advice. Intercourse could be discouraged; under the circumstances, it could not be stopped.

Late one winter afternoon, a sledge pulled up at our door. No one got out and two of us went to see why. In the sledge a youngish woman lay unconscious; huddled in sheepskins, she shook with ague. Later we learnt that she was driving from one distant village to another when the horse, no longer feeling her hand on the reins, took a turning that led to the hospital : as a foal it had been stabled at the agent's house. We put up the woman for the night, and I had to look after her. At day-break she woke with a great pain in her bowels and feeling very weak. Yet she firmly refused my humbly proffered assistance ; so presently we tottered down the slippery, narrow garden path. The hard snow underfoot was worn oily by the tread of shuffling feet. On either side, piled walls of a softer snow rose shoulder-high. Earth, air, and sky, void of colour, showed delicate gradations of white, grey, and black. Familiar shapes, faintly etched, emerged out of a milky mist : sheds, outhouses, the fence ; then the dim ring of trees, immense, motionless, expectant—a giant Colosseum empty of men and yet alive, rich with the sap of life, throbbing with suppressed excitement. The frozen stillness hung unstirred.

Suddenly Kilina clutched at me, gasped and gaped. Straight ahead, beyond the pale streak of the fence, a pitch-black giant fir tree leapt towards us stretching far up into the steaming sky ; shafts of rays like moonlight shot out of it, throwing into relief great downward-sweeping ribs of various grey—the branches. The light seemed to issue from inside the tree, but the trunk remained velvet dark. Could it be the sun rising behind ? We faced east, but miles of tousled thicket blocked the way between tree and sun. " Father Serafim ! " exclaimed Kilina in a rapture, " a mark of pity, of comfort for you and me from him ; given to us through a redeemed creature, a redeemed tree ! "

I had heard of St. Serafim in my childhood, and knew in a vague way that our lumber forest, Temniki, and his forest, Sarov, were remainders of one that in the past entirely covered northern and central Russia. But this knowledge was overlaid with more recent reading which had taught me that up to the twelfth century—when the Rus, or Russians of the Dnieper, began to migrate northeast—the forestland was inhabited by primitive Finnish tribes. Versed in practical Shamanism, magic and witchcraft, the Forest Finns lived in small groups and fought the wolf, the bear, and the wild cat for the possession of cave and thicket. The Rūs penetration being friendly on the whole, the Finns accepted baptism and merged with the newcomers who were chiefly of Slav and Scandinavian stock. The assimilation led to the Finns imprinting their Mongol characteristics on the mind and features of the mixed issue. But some isolated groups persistently refused intercourse; their descendants—who roused in the Christian majority feelings of contempt and awe—continued even in the twentieth century to live apart, in poor heathen hamlets. These primitive people were credited with an innate and traditional ability to capture and use to their own ends the forces of nature; and it was rumoured that they kept alive in " Holy Russia " an evil influence, hidden and all pervading. Our lumbermen—a mixed crowd—often alluded to the " evil hangover " that haunted the forest. Since my arrival I, too, had sensed an evil presence, immediate though intangible.

From the morning when Kilina led me to the " redeemed tree " and interpreted its message to me, the darkness lifted. At every step, I met Serafim. Wherever I went, whatever I did, whomever I nursed, all spoke of him. I learnt that Temniki and Sarov merged some thirty miles away; despite the impenetrable thicket between us we were neighbours according to local ideas, he and I. Stories of his life—detailed, vivid, intimate—poured into my eager ears, the story-tellers often amplifying a portrait with witty impersonations. I was impressionable at the time: words and impersonations remained branded on my memory.

When I left Russia, new friends who did not know the

popular legends spoke of Serafim in a way that was new to me : they had studied the written records. Disagreement on several points led me to consult the official biographies, and my preference for the floating tradition was confirmed. The recorded tradition, selected and expurgated at the saint's canonization, seems of less importance* than the oral : it does not present a connected story ; and it does not explain, as the floating tradition attempts to, the significance of Serafim for Russia. The floating tradition, which I have attempted to render, has preserved the tang of direct spiritual experience ; it discloses the mind of the people who keep it alive, contains incidents of human appeal and homely detail rich in local colour, and establishes Serafim a " local " Russian saint of unique, nation-wide significance.

Russia is a land of many saints, all are revered by her people but local saints, hardly known outside their own district, are surrounded with the greatest tenderness. This is due, above all, to the people's certainty that evil is everywhere present in their midst, and their gratitude to those who fight it and strive to make good prevail. Since the tenth century, when Christianity superseded paganism, man's ability to throw in his weight on the side of good or evil has been taken for granted ; and even in districts which have no " primitive " communities, a local need has been felt of saintly lives to counteract the evil lurking in nearby " plague-patches" and fostered by village witches. (Only of recent years has the psychological setting been modified, by collectivisation drives where they resulted in the removal of whole villages from one region to another.) A plague-patch can be situated on a hill or in a hollow, by a bog or on a clearing. The sinister event which first marked out the site is often obscured by tales of more recent crimes ; evil-doers gather there and keep alive the tradition of dis-

* Motovilov's memoirs, written much as the legend tellers speak, are an exception.

repute. Honest men avoid such places; they shun un toward encounters, and some have been unnerved to see their horse or dog show signs of distress—indeed of panic— when forced to enter a plague-patch; moreover the peasant, inclined to doze when jogging along at twilight or in the midday heat, believes that even the best people are exposed to destructive influences if, while asleep, they enter a place saturated with evil. Before the revolution, in many villages, men and women suspected of being witches lived alone or in pairs, usually in the last hut—least open to observation. The couples were often father and daughter or mother and son, seldom father and son or mother and daughter, and never, it would seem, husband and wife. Apparently only one household at a time was suspected of witchcraft, and the village commune—the *mir*—could easily have made life too difficult for the witches to continue there; but concerted action or drastic measures were seldom used, partly for fear of direct retaliation but also owing to the advantage felt in facing focussed evil, less fearsome than elusive evil which remains dispersed, without form or name, experienced but unseen. The tradition of witchcraft, mostly traceable in the last resort to the Forest Finns, continues in a steady thin stream, but covens are unknown, and there was no *grand siècle* of witch baiting. On the whole, Russian witches are lone wolves—lone were-wolves—though Alexei Tolstoi has fixed in a gruesome poem the tale of seven, hunting together on still, frosty nights; and the Bald Hill near Kiev is the eastern Brocken. Local plague-patches and village witches were for long the immediate concern of the peasant. And the pious lives of local saints—mostly monks or nuns who had led the regular religious life in the monasteries of the district or followed the somewhat anarchical way of the anchorite—were deemed the surest remedy. It was for the purifying, sweetening influence of their sanctity on the neighbourhood that local saints were cherished with an intimate gratitude, absent from the veneration of more exalted saints of universal Orthodox appeal. The part which monasteries may have played in achieving or maintaining national unity, spreading civilization, fostering agriculture, or doing good works, was little known and not greatly appreciated; much of the support given to local monasteries was due to their housing and training local fighters on the side of good. But material support and decoration of church and shrine could not fully satisfy the affection of the people for their saint; and the surplus overflowed into popular legends which often adorned the saint even in his lifetime. Into garlands of legend the people worked their reverent attempts intuitively to penetrate lives deemed more exposed to attacks by evil than their own; and they disclosed in them understanding of a mystical way which was believed hard and dangerous. Russians, nurtured on Isaiah, do not doubt that evil is created by the Lord, as peace is made by Him; they incline to think that man's capacity for evil grows with his capacity for God; and that in every generation it is the contemplatives—men and women experiencing an awareness which is neither of thought nor of the emotions—who are tempted most severely, in ways unimagined by other people. But the overcoming of such temptations makes them advance Godward, and those who have the vocation must courageously face the anguish. They do not stand alone, unaided. No one is, nor could anyone be, tempted as was Our Lord. And Christ is as near the tempted mind as He is to the broken heart.

Serafim of Sarov (1759-1833), who was called Prokhor Moshnin before he became a monk, is a typical local saint; but the whole of Russia is his field, and he fights everywhere for the nation's good against the nation's evil; everywhere and in all circumstances he sustains those who throw in their weight on the side of good. And when life is ugly and temptations appear to surpass men's powers of resistance, many Russians find help in considering the life of a Russian and almost a contemporary whose steadfastness overcame the greatest temptation—the revolt of an imaginative mind inspired by a compassionate heart. This temptation is omitted in the official biographies, but the legend makes it into a garland, and affectionately re-affirms Serafim a " local " saint.

Beside being a saint, Serafim was a *starets*, and much of the significance of his story to Russians lies in the simplicity to which he finally attained and which is in accordance with the Eastern Fathers' rendering of the way to " the life to come "—the life that is resurrection. The Fathers' ideal of the future life dwells in the subconscious of most, even unbelieving, Russians. One of the similies for it is a universal chorale directed towards God. There are as many " parts " as there are resurrected men, women, and " creatures." The part of every human being is unique. Only God knows a man's part before the man himself has learnt it through facing and overcoming his temptations. In prayer, particularly in the prayer described as " intercourse from mouth to ear," every one can learn from God the interpretation of his own part; but God's purpose often appears incredible to all except the person concerned. Therefore every one must be left spiritually free : free to follow God's inscrutable intentions. No one may interfere, few dare interpret. But if, through contemplation, a man attains to a particular kind of nearness to God, and comes to hear God's own interpretation of His word, and to perceive God's purpose for every one of His creatures, that man becomes a *starets*, a spiritual director. Such is the purpose set for him by God. In a sense this is a personal tragedy : uninterrupted contemplation is man's greatest delight, but those who seek it run the risk of being chosen to give love as lavishly (according to human capacity) as it has been given to them. Love, kindled in them by their nearness to God, leads them back to men. They can no longer dwell in unbroken beatitude. But since love is Christ's, and Christ-like action renders present the Comforter who is joy, those who, for love of their brethren, leave the delight of contemplation, attain to joy in the Holy Ghost. The outward sign of this grace is a great simplicity, chief mark of the Russian *starets*.

Simplicity, profoundly admired by Russians, is thought by them to be a distinctively Russian virtue; which must astonish anyone but themselves. And yet an attentive study of Russia shows them to be right. True, the idiom used by Russians is mostly the complicated conventional phraseology of the day; rococo, romantic, or Red. The pattern of their discourses and trend of thought—or, in the case of a novelist like Dostoievskii, the characters they create and the situations they construe are involved, even chaotic. But through the surface of elaborate clichès and through the subsoil of untidy thoughts and uncouth actions, there break nether themes of classical simplicity; themes born of a spirit aware that diversities are right and therefore rendered one in God. None can explain multiplicity in unity. But the simple man is aware that when he dares to delve deep enough, he sees his faith grounded in reality and hears the Word which solves all riddles. He has approached the source of his simplicity.

Russians, stifled by the conventions of their idiom and distracted by the chaos of their thought and feelings, find consolation and encouragement in considering the life of Serafim, who was one of them and attained to the simplicity of a selfless personality. Men of other countries may find the enigma of Russia easier to understand if they perceive the Russians' reverence for the simplicity of the humblest among them; it is a key to much that appears baffling to the Western mind.

I GODWARD BOUND

The highest perfection of a thing is to be subject to that which perfects it.

THE CALL

ENGLAND and France were fighting beyond the Atlantic. Europe was enduring the Seven Years War, and Russia was taking part in it. The usually sleepy little town of Kursk—two hundred and fifty miles south of Moscow and two hundred and fifty east of Kiev—had entered its short yearly period of sleepless nights; in this part of Russia, St. Elijah always ushers in a period of heavy storms.

It had been sultry all day. The evening was oppressively still. Agatha—wife of Isidor Moshnin, merchant-builder—leaning heavily on the banisters which she clutched with her right hand, slowly mounted the dimly lit, narrow wooden staircase of their comfortable home.

Suddenly a great gust rushed at the outer walls; whistled round corners; swept over the roof. A loose tile, torn out of place, slipped down the steep incline; fell; broke with a piteous short clang. A distant rumble growled and slowly died down, rendering the renewed silence even more still.

She pressed her left hand to her side. The birth pangs were becoming more frequent and growing more difficult to bear. Better call Auntie from her room up in the dormers. Tiresome. They had hoped it would be to-morrow, in daylight. Still, they could get things ready quickly, the two of them, while she was able to move about. But first she must have a peep at Alexis. Four years old. Such a big boy.

With tousled fair hair and flushed round face, the child lay on his side, one chubby fist tightly wedged between his full lips. Twice he sucked loudly. Then sighed tremulously and dropped into even deeper sleep. Agatha re-adjusted the bed-clothes and crept out. At the door she doubled up. Head swimming, she leant against the door post.

A streak of lightning illumined the landing. Ghostly white it flashed in at a small window that had neither curtain nor shutter. A loud peal followed.

Auntie, a portly figure draped in a voluminous much-washed dressing-gown, tying a sprigged kerchief round her head and muttering snatches of prayers and incantations, came tumbling down from her room. Catching sight of the young woman, she threw up her hands, " It would be so ! Just as the storm is closing in upon us. Get to your room, child. I'll send the girl for the Old Woman." Her long brown plait, streaked with grey, dangled far below the edges of her kerchief. It swung a little, right and left, as she bustled downstairs.

The girl, a robust fourteen-year-old who slept by the kitchen, was somewhat rudely shaken out of her first sleep. Delighted, as all women old or young are at the news of a marriage or a birth, she pattered off down the street, hurrying to get back before the storm broke.

Alive to the dignity of the moment, Aunt Martha advanced toward the study; stopped; pursed her lips; theatrically drew back the curtain. Isidor sat at a large table, head propped up with both hands. His long fingers moved slowly, gently rubbing his scalp through dark hair, thick and long. By the dim light of an oil lamp, he pored over one of Rastrelli's plans of a Russian church. What a genius the Italian was. Now that Isidor had seen this, no other would do for the new church of St. Sergius. He'd make a gem of it. Better than any other thing he had ever built.

Auntie cleared her throat. Isidor looked up quickly and guessed her errand. " Now you just sit quite still and don't worry," she said excitedly, " everything is all right. I'll see to everything. Everything will be quite all right."

" Yes, yes, yes," he agreed ; rose and passed her ; mounted the stairs two steps at a time ; entered the bedroom on tiptoe, in a vain effort to muffle the creaking of his boots.

Agatha, still dressed, lay across the bed. Approaching, he patted her cheek, lately grown pale and hollow ; muttered, " Courage, my pet," bent down and kissed her on the brow. It was cold and damp.

Crossing her aunt on the landing, he mumbled, " M-hm!" and nodded thoughtfully ; then stopped and whispered, " I'll tell the yard-servant to stoke the bath house." " He's doing so already ! " she looked at him reproachfully over her shoulder. Stroking his beard, he returned to the study and Rastrelli's beautiful church. But while he clearly visualized all the details of the building, he strained his ears to catch the significance of every sound that drifted down to him. He was twenty years her elder. They married before she was seventeen. Death always hovers over a birth. What would he do if she left him ? How bring up Alexis ? Try and keep Auntie there for ever ? But she was such a fuss-pot and would get entirely out of hand without Agatha's steadying influence. And the Newcomer ? What would he do about him ? Or her ? Get a nurse ? Marry again ? Couldn't think of it. They had been quietly happy for five years. What was that ? Ah, the Old Woman, at last. " Mother of God, protect the woman of this house. I'll pour all my gratitude into St. Sergius if . . ."

The wind was howling and whirling without a break. Somewhere a large shutter knocked incessantly. He got up in search of it. As he stood by a window, making it fast, a great flash cut through the opaque darkness, zigzagging to earth. Blinded, he started back. A crash of thunder overhead deafened him to every other sound.

"Must have hit something, that one. God grant it's not a human dwelling." Torrents of rain came pouring down.

Upstairs Agatha had been tossing and moaning for what seemed to her a very long time. "Do open the window," she gasped, "it's stifling."

"Be reasonable," Auntie remonstrated, "the wind would blow out the light. What should we do then?"

"It would lift the roof off our heads, dearie," the Old Woman put in, "lift the roof, destroy us all and the precious new life too."

As blinding lightning rent the night, and thunder crashed down on their heads, they cowered. "The mercy of heaven preserve us," gasped the girl. Agatha turned her head and looked at them silently, severely. Guiltily, all three bent over the bed. The new life squealed piteously; so small a voice after the boisterous thunder. It was August 1, 1759.

A few weeks later, the second son of Isidor Moshnin was christened and given the name of Prokhor. He was a happy baby and very quiet; no trouble at all.

Late in autumn news reached Kursk that Auntie's youngest son, Misha, had fallen in a great battle near Frankfurt on the Oder. The Russians and their Austrian allies had caught Frederick of Prussia off his guard, mauled his army and artillery, caused him hastily to retreat. Then, grown indolent, they gave him time to recover; and he hit back. But Misha would never recover or return.

Auntie's other children, five of them, were married and settled in different towns of Central Russia. Wrapped in her youngest, alone still with her, she had become somewhat of a stranger to the rest. So the Moshnins suggested she should sell or let her house and share their life. There was lots to do with two small children about.

While she was away, autumn slush changed to winter

snow. The nights, grown long, glittered with stars. The days, though bright, were short.

With the cold, Isidor's kidney complaint unexpectedly returned; it was fifteen years since his last relapse. Having lost the habit of pain and discomfort, he grumbled when Agatha was not by his side and wished to goodness Auntie was through with that house of hers and back minding the children. In the meantime, Alexis spent many hours with Yakov the yard-servant and Niusha the girl; he was running wild.

Whenever Isidor was at home, in his study, Agatha would take Prokhor out of his cot, wrap him in his shawls, go downstairs with him and, putting the child in the corner of a large divan, sit down in the armchair that waited for her by the writing desk.

From the first weeks of their married life, she had shown interest in her husband's work. Admiring her taste, he soon came to discuss the more attractive, artistic side with her, and to ask her advice on many points. But now, she quickly acquired a sound knowledge of business details and gladly helped him with the dull office work. She was apparently keen to learn that part of the business which increasingly bored the master builder.

After concentrating for a while on the estimates and figures, Isidor would take the St. Sergius sketches and plans out of their drawer and go into ecstasies over the proportions.

"Just look, Aggie, look at the dome. No weight at all— so perfect a part of the whole building! And the belfry. That gradual inward slope on all sides as it rises. What perfection."

He tore himself away from it at last. Then caught sight of his son staring at him wide-eyed, looking very wise. Isidor's face, which in its tautness had resembled that of a fiery prophet, relaxed into great wrinkles of tenderness.

"Look!" he exclaimed softly, "he understands, he's listening. Oh, he'll be a great architect, this son of ours. Alexis'll take on the business but this one we'll send to Moscow, Petersburg, abroad. To Italy! He'll be a great builder of churches. The whole world will ring with his fame. The world of Lutherans and Papists as well as our own. Isn't that so, Sonny?" and he clicked his tongue at him.

Agatha lightly crossed the room. Her gently swaying, full skirts underlined the re-acquired slimness of her waist. "We must be careful," she said, "not to keep him awake when he's down here. They need sleep as we need air; when they're so young." Lifting the child, she turned him right round. He faced a blank and uninteresting wall. For a few minutes he crooned and gurgled happily, then fell asleep.

When Auntie returned—with many boxes and even some of her favourite furniture—she took over Alexis and the house-keeping. Agatha devoted herself to Prokhor, Isidor, and Isidor's work. Presently, under her husband's guidance, she was running the whole business, except for the building of St. Sergius. The office boy, the foreman, and the workmen got used to taking their orders from her; the master's orders, of course; she was only his mouthpiece; but she did know what she was talking about.

She would gladly have done much more to lighten the burden she saw weighing him down. When he was not engrossed in St. Sergius, he increasingly worried over the fate of the country. What, he wondered, was life coming to? Not his own or the children's—these were safe in Agatha's hands—but the life of their unhappy country. Why had the eighteen years of respite not continued? How he had rejoiced at the coronation of Tsar Peter's daughter, Elizabeth, coming as she did after all these other battling, Germanizing successors of his.

Lovely and fearless, she had started boldly—a great

Empress! On a night when the throne or the convent were a toss up for her, she at last evaded the vigilance of "the Brunswicks' German Courtiers," and suddenly appeared at the barracks of the valiant *Preobrazhentsi*.* Swayed by tender enthusiasm, she and the Guardsmen took oaths of eternal mutual fidelity. The Guards stood for the Russian people that night, and she had won.

Some said she was frivolous, bored by the business of running a State; that she was dissolute; only danced and sang; wore fancy dress (a man's coat and breeches) more often than decent clothes; gave extravagant parties that cost as much as a good battle might. Maybe, maybe—God save her soul. We're all sinners, every one of us—but for fifteen years there had been no wars. Let her dance, bless her pretty little feet. The whole country was steadily recovering, growing more prosperous; even the deadly clamps of bureaucracy were being loosened here and there.

But things had gone wrong lately. Why was the country at war again? Russia had nothing to gain by participating in a European squabble. This was no holy war. And yet her young men were dying abroad, and in the country conditions were deteriorating. Elizabeth was growing old. The Russian Sun-Empress was sinking fast.

She had a stroke some time ago, and no wonder. Why had she, she of all people, brought that under-developed, puny German nephew into the country, and made him heir? Married him to a wanton German princess too; not to a sensible Russian girl, as was done of old.

Not that Isidor was a stickler, an Old Believer. No, he approved of development, was thrilled by growth, by the birth of a child, the return of spring. But this new-fangled Germanization was neither growth nor renewal. Elizabeth had rightly fought against its spreading in the country. But—that nephew of hers.

* A regiment created by her father and devoted to his memory.

She should have kept out of the European war. But since she had not, surely all must support her? But no, the Holstein Monkey and his disreputable Consort had set up a Young Court in opposition to the Old. They idolized Frederick, whom Russia was fighting. Some even said they were his spies; informed the enemy of Elizabeth's intentions; turned her army's victories to nought: none of these were ever followed up, no advantage was ever gained by Russia, no matter how dearly she paid in lives and money. Poor country. The country his sons would live in; ruled by the Holstein Monkey.

In Isidor's mood of despondency, Agatha and St. Sergius were his only sources of consolation. But as the days grew longer and the warmer wind was laden with promise, his dark mood lifted. As soon as the snow was melted and the earth had dried, they would be clearing the site for the crowning work of his life; laying the foundations. Thanks to Agatha, he could entirely devote himself to St. Sergius. What a gem he'd make of it.

In April, he felt much better. Soon he would be sending to Simovo for that herb. It had cured him last time and kept the ailment down for all these years. It would be at its best, its most potent, in July. He remembered the herballist telling him so.

But, late in May, he got a worse attack than he had ever had; it weakened his heart, and he died, in great pain, on the twenty-third.

Even the death of a child affects a household profoundly. In a family—that supra-personal unit where every personality counts—the unit is no longer the same when any one personality drops out. The rebuilding of the bereaved, truncated body is a slow and painful re-adjustment.

Auntie, still dazed by the loss of her son and the cardinal change it had brought into her life, moved about like an automaton, wound up perilously tight. She was more erect than usual, her thin little eyebrows rose high on her corrugated forehead, the pitch of her voice was that of a sleep walker's.

But Agatha had grown even more calm and low voiced than usual. The exhausting burial ceremonies over, she asked Auntie to come into the study while Niusha minded the boys.

" I know," she started without preamble, " I know, dear, that I can count on you taking full charge of the house and children."

" Children ? "

" Yes. Prokhor will have to be weaned at once. I'm taking over the business, it will require all my time and thought, in the first year or two."

" The business ! You, a woman, so young, you can't."

" I must. God brought you to our house so that I might. I see His will clearly. It's only a matter of ten years or so, till Alexis can begin to learn from me what I've learnt from Isidor. It's God's will ; we must obey Him." She bent down, lightly kissed her bewildered aunt, and went up to her room.

There was no protest when the burly master-builder's wife, small, slight, with a gentle manner and direct steady gaze, took full command. Had she not been doing much the same for half a year ? Besides, in the first days, her bereavement nipped in the bud any of the cruder banter that might have hovered in the workmen's minds. And by the time the family tragedy had lost its poignancy, she was well established in their esteem. Having got accustomed to the new situation, they accepted it as a matter of course. Busy days ran smoothly.

News of what happened at Court, and even in Europe, got round the country with remarkable speed, considering the state of the roads and the lack of all desire in high places that the people should know anything. But there were the Country Houses : their owners had cousins or uncles at Court and in the Army, and all had servants who were of the people. News did get around ; all of it ; though sordid scandal travelled quickest.

Towards Christmas—the first not presided over by Isidor in the Moshnins' home—they heard of the October raid on Berlin. With drums, songs, and music, the Russian Army entered the Prussian capital, enforced a levy, looted the shops, got gloriously drunk, enjoyed themselves for three grand days, and then marched out again to more music, songs, and drums. As usual, nothing came of it. But it did make a good story for a soldier to tell his sons if he ever got back from the fighting which followed in Pomerania.

The next Christmas, however, was dismal. The Empress lay sick, very sick. On January 2, 1762, Elizabeth died. By this time Frederick's army could no longer offer serious resistance. If Russia and Austria at last co-ordinated their actions, he would be smashed. But the new Tsar, Peter III—the Holstein Monkey—sent declarations of loyalty to his idol, and put his army, the Russian Army, at the feet of the King of Prussia : to be used by him when, how, and against whom he wished. Austria, perhaps ?

The dazed country was relieved at the end of war, but amazed at the unusual way of bringing about peace. Amazement soon changed to bitter resentment. Not because of peace with the foreigner, but because of the trend of things at home : the gentry were emancipated from their life-long compulsory service to the State, emancipated from it all. But their privileges, that sprung from that service, were retained, even enhanced. Was it fair ?

In July, Sophia of Anhalt-Zerbst, wife of Peter III, deposed him and ascended the throne as Catherine II of Russia. Her popularity could never fall as low as his. He, the " impotent profligate," was hated more than any other had ever been. Her reign could not be worse; would it be better?

Prokhor was almost four, Alexis eight. The two boys, Agatha and Auntie had spent the day, a Sunday, at the cemetery beyond the Old Church. Isidor's grave was bright with flowers. As they were leaving, two heavy storm clouds, speeding towards each other from east and west, burst overhead. With a shuddering roar, amid thunder and lightning, torrents of rain came pouring down. The Moshnins sought shelter in a chapel, on the way to the gates. It smelt of incense and votary candles. Prokhor sniffed the air reflectively, grew very silent, and angered Alexis by refusing to take part in any game. There was no one else for the bigger boy to play with; Auntie began a long, long story about a wolf, a fox, and a hare. Agatha sat down and took Prokhor on her knee.

The storm passed as quickly as it had come. Below the chapel steps a large puddle filled a dip in the sand path. There were more puddles beyond. This was the shortest way to the gates, but it lay lower than the rest. Alexis was promptly sent away from the temptation to splash through water. He, the hare, was to run down another path, longer but drier; Auntie, the wolf, followed.

Agatha, holding Prokhor in her arms, gingerly stepped over the puddle where it was narrowest. The air was very clear, very still and cool. Drooping branches of silver birch hung motionless; their leaves shone emerald bright. Straight ahead, two perfect rainbows gleamed on a dark blue, fathomless sky. Birds chirped gaily.

From behind one of the trees, there stepped a ragged figure drenched to the bone and, apparently, not minding it. Slight of build, young, pale, unkempt, unshaven, unwashed, and untidy, he looked at Agatha with a wild fixed stare. Her heart gave a great leap. It was Grisha the Fool. She had always feared him.

"Back at last from your long pilgrimage, Grisha," she remarked in a flat voice holding Prokhor tighter. But he was in no mood to listen, " Do not let the fire scorch your flesh, your pale cool flesh," he shouted. " Put it down, let it be, woman ! Once it was yours to hold and tend, it is yours no longer. Let it be. The flame shall rise, as rise it must, rise to its Creator, One in Three and Three in One. The flaming prayer shall rise, and grace will rain down upon the world of sin. Put it down, put it down, woman ! "

He was in one of his dangerous moods. Agatha had known him use the foulest language when this came upon him. She ran down the path as quickly as she could with Prokhor in her arms. At the gate she put him down, and joined Alexis and Auntie who had heard the shouting but not the words. These never made sense anyway. " But they really are dangerous and terrifying these fools, when young, while their blood still burns in them," Auntie complained. " They gain insight when it cools, I know, but I don't like them, I'm glad I came the other way."

That night Prokhor had a fever. Fearfully Agatha wondered if Grisha had meant him by the fire, and foretold his death. " Let it be . . . once it was yours . . . it is yours no longer . . . let it rise to its Creator."

They sprinkled him with holy water, gave him some of it to drink, had an intercessory service said for him. He lay in a stupor for more than a week asking for nothing, never focussing anything when his eyes were open. Then slowly he began to recover.

Soon Alexis was allowed, then encouraged, to come into the sick room and play with his brother. But a gulf seemed to have opened between them. Prokhor was engrossed in remembering the Gates. Gates of Gold that led to light. They were the one thing that mattered now ; but no words he knew could encompass his vision or express his yearning. He kept silent ; turned to the wall, sighed and thought.

When he was strong enough to get up and take part in the family life, Agatha spent as much of her time as was possible, with the children. Always on Sunday afternoons, and sometimes during the week, she would tell them stories out of the lives of saints. After this, they were allowed to play quietly, while she read the Gospels, Epistles, or Acts to Auntie and Niusha.

Alexis, sitting on the floor, would amuse himself cutting houses out of cardboard. They were good models. Niusha sometimes helped. But Prokhor remained beside Agatha, nestling to her side. The Gates were nearer when he sat like this.

During that winter, the house was full of visitors, mostly needy ones whom Agatha gathered under her wing. If they chanced to come while she was telling her stories or reading, they too, sat down and listened. The house was acquiring a reputation and respect it had never enjoyed before.

In time, all traces of Prokhor's illness vanished. He again took part in his big brother's games, and when they went out for their long rambles with Yakov the yard-servant, listened, entranced, to all the old man had to say about birds and animals, bees and plants.

As the children grew older, the years passed more quickly. St. Sergius, a large brick and stucco church, was nearing completion. Its pilasters, columns, architraves, and ornament gleamed snowy white against a painted glowing strawberry-pink background. The townsfolk were proud of their new church and of their townswoman, the admirable widow of Isidor the Builder.

It was Prokhor's seventh birthday. As part of her present to him, Agatha had long ago promised to take him up on to the belfry, right to the top of it. They started out together immediately after the midday meal. Prokhor was excited and talked all the way. Would she teach him how to read ? Would she herself teach him ? No, not Alexis, nor his teacher, the Lector ; she herself. It would make it easier, quicker. Then as he grew a little older, whenever she rested on the big divan in the study, he'd read to her the tales of the Desert Fathers, which they both liked so much : The one about the little fawn that wept with joy when he met a kind old hermit in the grim harsh land of rocks ; and the one about the lions that carefully buried their lifelong friend, Abbot Paul ; and the one about the birds that brought food to the solitaries.

They had reached the church, and the foreman was waiting for them by the corkscrew stairway that led to the top of the belfry. The higher they went, the slower they moved ; it was a steep ascent. At last, right up, they came out into the open, on to a platform still roofless and thick with scaffolding. Here the great bells would, eventually, hang.

"Be careful where you step. Mind your head," said the man to Agatha. "This," he added, "is what I meant the other day : the lower end of the Great Bell shouldn't come below this, see ? And . . ."

Feeling that Prokhor had left her side, Agatha turned round quickly. He was at the very edge. No—over. With a hollow cry, she clasped her head with both hands ; was sinking to the untidy dusty floor ; no, flying like the wind down the endless, twisting corkscrew. The heavy, unwieldy foreman clattered after her, unable to keep pace.

God, how would she find him, what would he look like. On and on, round and round, down and down. The ground floor at last. She bolted past a leisurely group of workmen ; rushed out of the huge doors ; stopped, rooted to the ground. How warm the sun was on her head and shoulders. How gentle the wind on her face.

Prokhor stood only a few paces away, on the dusty white road, examining with great attentiveness a large heap of rubble : dust, shavings, chips of ruddy brick and grey stones.

" Prokhor ! "

" You know," he said coming up to her, a perplexed expression on his suntanned face, " I fell ! But the Queen of the Skies spread her cloak under me and we floated down ; like kites, when the wind drops. It was there," pointing to a heap, " it was there just now, so blue. I got up, but it was gone ; where is it now ? " He gazed up at her with a puzzled frown.

Agatha took his face in her hands. " Gathered in your eyes." She had never seen them so dark. Gleaming cornflowers under the ruffled shock of fair hair, golden as ripening corn.

At a little distance, the foreman and his workmen gaped. " The Holy Cross preserve us," muttered one of them, under his breath, " Fallen from such a height and not a bone broken. The Lord must love him ! "

Hand in hand, more joyous even than on their way to the belfry, mother and son returned home to partake of yet another birthday meal.

That winter, Prokhor put all his heart into his lessons. Toward spring, he could be found, at all hours, in the study pouring over his mother's books ; slowly deciphering them. During the summer the Lector took him over from Agatha, and soon Prokhor added to his old favourites new ones, books on houses and ships, off his father's shelf.

The business was flourishing. Agatha could and would send their youngest to Moscow or Petersburg ; perhaps Italy, as Isidor had wished. He would be a great architect. Alexis, much slower but very steady and practical, would be his business manager. An ideal partnership. The boys were great friends.

In these days, many new books were being published in

St. Petersburg and Moscow. New poets and writers in prose were being spoken of. An entirely new, cheap, and topical kind of reading could be had too : journalism was spreading ; spreading even to the provinces. Alexis was keen on this newer reading, and, to the delight of their neighbours, Agatha kept him well provided with it.

Again there was fighting. In the North, in Poland, Russia waged a war that was not called by that name because Catherine's troops were there to protect King Stanislas from his insurgent subjects. He had asked for her help, she was giving it. If she readily gave more than he asked, that came of her generous nature. While she was thus engaged, the Crimean Tartars, subjects of the Sultan of Turkey, attacked the Russian borderland more successfully than usual. The Russians hit back ; also more successfully than usual. There resulted a Turkish war ; one of many. Then, Frederick of Prussia enquired of his cousin Catherine if she did not think a partition of Poland—that never knew her own mind—a good idea ?

By this time, in the general excitement, Prokhor was picking up anything in print, reading it avidly, and discussing it at length with the Lector, Alexis, Agatha, Auntie, or any one of the constant visitors. His memory was remarkable, his mind clear, his judgment keen, and his thirst for knowledge insatiable.

This proved his undoing. About three years after the incident in the belfry, he fell seriously ill. A well known leech, passing through their town, was called to his bedside and put down the indisposition to mental overstrain. He bled the boy, and prescribed hot mustard foot baths to draw what blood there remained in him away from the head.

It didn't help. Prokhor grew weaker. The local bonesetter, the apothecary from the Church Square, and the Old Woman who had presided over his birth, all came in turns. All shook their heads, shrugged their shoulders, and could think of nothing but more bleeding and more footbaths. Poultices too, perhaps.

Agatha was in despair. Late one night, as she hovered over him, he opened his eyes and looked at her with a new directness. In the dim light of the sanctuary lamp before the ikons in the corner of the room, his eyes were very large and dark. " I'll get well, Mama," he said, " the Queen of the Skies bade me tell you. I dreamt a jumble of things. Then all tidied itself; in the quiet she came. Said, ' I'll visit you soon, and you'll get well. Tell your mother. She mustn't worry.' "

Agatha kissed him and went to bed reassured. Rooted in the old faith of her people, she could not doubt St. Mary's willingness to help, and took for granted the accuracy of her child's simple rendering. Patiently she waited for the Grace of God to visit their home.

As most Russian monasteries, the Kursk monastery of the Revelation of Our Lady harboured within its walls a miraculous ikon—a focal point of the Presence, a point in space where the Presence had come to rest. It was a Virgin and Child painted in tempera on wood. The possession of this ikon was shared by the Kursk Monastery and the Anchorhold of the Roots, built in 1597 in a thick dark wood, through which flowed the winding river Tuskora. Popular opinion had it that, at the end of the thirteenth century, the painting was found on this spot, by the river, firmly wedged between the great roots of an old tree.

In memory of this event, every year on the ninth Sunday after Easter, the ikon was carried in a procession to the Anchorhold, whence it returned with the same ceremonies and pageantry to its winter quarters, on the twelfth of September.

That September opened with a spell of March weather;

brilliant sunshine preceded and followed streaming rain; gusts of wind sprang up from nowhere, tore round street corners and suddenly died down. The chanting procession, with its bright banners swaying high up on gilded poles, tramped past the Moshnins' house. As a drenching shower came pouring down, "Take the short cut," someone shouted in a powerful bass, "the short cut through Moshnins' yard." It was customary in these days that anyone whose holding could offer a short cut to some much frequented place, should open his yard to the public for this use. Isidor had done so long before his marriage, but few people availed themselves of the privilege.

Now, two women at the head of the procession pushed open the yard gate, and all jostled in. The downpour increased. Agatha had been standing by Prokhor's window. As quick as thought, she gathered him in her arms. Light as a feather! There was no flesh on his bones, and no weight to his body, grown long and frighteningly thin.

When she stepped out on to the yard porch, the ikon, surrounded by banner bearers, was taking cover there. The rest of the procession was already reforming. Agatha, with Prokhor in her arms, bowed low before St. Mary and begged a blessing. On the way out, the ikon was carried over the whole length of the sick boy's emaciated body. The Mother and Child were leaving; the short visit was over. Smiling, Agatha and Prokhor looked into each other's eyes: the Queen of Heaven had come; a turning point was reached, the days of anguish were over; days of joy drew near.

As soon as Prokhor could sit up in bed, he asked for pencils and a drawing pad. For hours he dreamt over it; then, carefully began to build, with pencil on paper, the Church of the Holy Mother.

He had come to a decision, and knew now that it had been maturing for many years. Because of it his recovery was a dedication. A dedication to the light beyond the Gates. He would unflinchingly serve the power which expressed itself in that light. The power which was always by his side, spreading a blue mantle under him to change his fall to a gentle flight, sending to his house the Supreme Intercessor, alone capable of revivifying his ailing body which could now harbour his spirit for many years to come. He dedicated himself as its servant; and his dedication was silent as that of a servant should be.

Since he was to be an architect, his service would take the form of building churches, God's mansions. He would build them as the monks painted ikons of old: praying, fasting, meditating on them in silence. He would refuse to build anything else, no matter how tempting an offer was made to him.

He told no one of his dedication. It was a secret between him and his Master. His will had been touched by that of Another. The mystery was too sacred to be hardened into words.

He discovered in his heart a golden realm of perfect quiet. When—at play or at work—he stopped and turned his gaze inward, he smiled inundated with light. Agatha did not question him. But, when she saw him smile, a reflection of his radiance made her glad.

THE WAY

NEXT year there appeared at Kursk Ivan Lukich, an original. This tall, thin, and sallow weed of a man was the last descendant of a dim and poor, landless family of Petrine gentry. But he had been given an unusual and expensive education by his godfather, who saw to it that Ivan mastered philosophy, metaphysics, and mathematics, French and the dancing of the minuet, German and the playing of the flute. For years Ivan had hung around his benefactor's house discussing subtle questions with foreign diplomats, dancing with their wives and daughters, and playing the flute to the accompaniment of his godfather's violin.

Then the old man died of a stroke, leaving his entire fortune to the Empress with a humble request that it should be used for the benefit of the St. Petersburg Academy of Arts. After some pulling of strings, two friends of the deceased secured for the disappointed godson a government post at Kursk and sent him off, glad to be rid of the absurd creature.

The government post was insignificant, the pay poor, but there was hope of promotion if Ivan kept away from the bottle; his father had died of D.T.

Lukich, as he was now called, went about Kursk as he had gone about St. Petersburg, seeking to impress on everyone the importance of finding the right method to obtain real knowledge.

"We must think, think for ourselves. Not deaden our minds by dull plodding through the minds of others or by repeating their assertions, parrot-pat. We must think, think, think. Then, in the core of our mind, we shall find the method. Certitude; infallible! Ma-the-ma-tical." Standing in the middle of a room he would declaim for hours, whether others listened or not. From time to time, he would tap his forehead, adjust his periwig with a nervous jerk, or brush off his pale blue sleeve flecks of snuff that were not there; he was meticulously tidy. His audience, none of whom read much, nodded their approval.

When, applying the mathematical method, he launched out into philosophical and metaphysical speculations and, having got inextricably entangled, plunged into the theory of the vortex, all crowded round, gasping with admiration.

Never had they dreamt of such wisdom; quite incomprehensible.

At fifteen years of age, Alexis was seriously preparing to share the burden of the business with his mother; Prokhor, in view of his future calling, required a sound knowledge of mathematics. Agatha got Lukich to come to the house three times a week : twice for both boys together and once for Prokhor alone.

One day, Alexis, always keenly attentive to what was going on around him and on the alert for new impressions, looked more carefully at the zigzag of a man seated by his side, and summed him up: " Growing very threadbare at the elbows, mothy about the wig, angular about the shoulders. Sunken eyes and hollow cheeks!"

" What a warm house!" Lukich exclaimed next time, crossing the threshold of the study. Then, sitting down by the table, " Why, what's this ? "

" Dull for you, I thought, while we plod on at our problems," Alexis said carelessly. " Munching whiles away the time."

Absentmindedly Lukich chewed the smoked goose and gulped down the kvas; his glassy grey eyes stared straight ahead into paradise regained : the chaos of metaphysics grown mathematically tidy through the efforts of Ivan Lukich.

Henceforth he was asked to stay to a meal at least once a week. At table he explained, with many a flourish of his long scraggy hand, the eternal fight between chaos and order.

Auntie had never met anyone like him; her thin little eyebrows rose very high. Her full pouting lips opened a little. She plied him with a second helping; then, with a third. His teeth were bad and he ate slowly.

" As thin as a scarecrow," she would sigh when he left. " But I do think he's looking a teeny bit more happy, a weeny bit less lost, don't you ? "

But on the days when Lukich and Prokhor, alone in the study, rose together to the heady heights of speculative thought, the tray of goose and kvas often remained untouched.

After his seventeenth birthday, Alexis could no longer devote any time at all to his education: he aimed at gradually taking the whole of the business off his mother's hands. Besides, he was in love.

Prokhor had Lukich to himself. They put aside all books, and spent their time thinking; thinking aloud; and arguing till the house rang with their excited voices and Auntie came pattering to the study door.

"Goodness gracious me," she would exclaim, drawing back the curtain, "I thought something had happened!"

"So there has, Lady?" replied Lukich rising and bowing, "the clash of two master minds."

Suddenly an upheaval, that gained momentum every week, shook the Russian Empire. An uncouth Cossack of sturdy build, insatiable appetites, crude humour, and keen wits, raised his banner—the banner of Holstein!—beyond the Iayik. Because of the rigours of Catherine's reign, even more peasants than usual had lately been "running away" to the east. Disgruntled and distressed, they rallied to the call: "We, Peter the Third, grant you full freedom and all our land to till. The landowners will be wiped out." In thousands they gathered round this man of their own stock who proclaimed himself their lawful Tsar. Catherine, he said, had attempted, but failed, to kill him.

"We will confine in a convent, for life, our unfaithful spouse, Catherine," he boasted.

In the meanwhile, as a mild temporary consolation, he instituted a College of Six Concubines, permanently attached to his Imperial Court. Since the Empress's numerous favourites were, at all times, conspicuous at hers, these six women were trundled all over Eastern Russia, wherever the engagement with Catherine's armies led her "sorely offended husband."

Emilian Pugachev's luck in the field was stupendous, his popularity among the peasants growing from day to day. True, his armies looted and burnt villages, destroyed property, raped women. But he set up tribunals on village greens and in town squares to deal with such cases. "It's the men; he himself has a sense of justice," the villagers concluded. For the rest, there was no redress for landlords, their wives and daughters; a new and better justice, indeed!

Already the Rabble Army had put the stronghold of Kazan to the torch, and was heading for Moscow. But Catherine having settled Polish and Turkish affairs, could at last devote her whole attention to crushing the impostor.

"Why?" moaned Lukich, in trepidation, "How is it, that such a grand effort is needed? I shudder, shudder, shudder to think how close we stand to the chasm of chaos. There it is, by our side, always, waiting to engulf the world; the world into which we are at such pains to bring order. How does this turbulent maniac gain battle after battle? How can it be that the whim of a madman can precipitate us into chaos? The Empress has strategists of great repute in her service. A strategist has the mind of a mathematician. The mind and the method. A chaotic urge cannot, must not defeat the clear, the lucid mind." He paced about the study in great agitation, tears streaming down his face.

"Or," he stopped, carefully wiping his eyes and looking round slyly, "or, is it that none of them has ever thought, thought for himself? Is it that they only recite the thoughts of others? Whereas he, the uncouth illiterate backwoodsman—*he thinks*," Lukich shouted suddenly. Then, laughing hysterically, poked his finger into Auntie's face as she came hurrying in, disturbed by new, strange, intonations in his voice.

After a moment of tense silence, " Lukich," she said, with a catch of commisseration in her voice, " Go home. You're not well."

He drew himself up in proud protest ; looked down into her puffy old face. It was neither haughty nor reproving ; full of understanding, distressed. Hanging his head guiltily and hunching his shoulders he slunk out.

" Drunk ! " exclaimed Prokhor under his breath. " Lukich, drunk ! "

From that day, no one knew when the Original might fail to come and give his lesson ; even fail to put in an appearance at the government office. He had slipped out of the realm of order that he pined for and adored. Chaos was master of his life.

On a warm day in early spring, Prokhor, having waited in vain for his teacher, wandered out to the cemetery. Deep in thought, he sat on the wooden bench by his father's grave. Pugachev and Lukich had broken the smooth ring of light in his heart. The surface was disturbed, dark eddies appeared here and there. He felt unhappy, restless.

Presently Grisha came slouching by ; stopped ; ambled up to the boy and sat down beside him. In the last years, the fool had changed. " His blood was cooling," Auntie would have said. Grown less violent, he was gaining wisdom and insight.

" The mind," he said, fiddling with his hands, " must humble itself to the heart. The mind is proud. It strays. Leads astray the weakling heart, lost to humility."

" I must know about things," mused Prokhor, as though speaking to himself. " I must know them clearly in my head, think about them clearly ; to do my work ; I've got to build churches."

"No, no. Not churches! Church."

Does he mean I shall never build more than one, thought Prokhor, dismayed. Why?

But, muttering and shrugging, Grisha was ambling away towards the gates.

At the Moshnins', Alexis and six other young men were heatedly discussing the latest news. Pseudo-Tsars, and even Pseudo-Pugachevs, were springing up everywhere. Proclaiming freedom, they spread terror throughout the country and ruthlessly deprived men, women and children, rich and poor, of every vestige of liberty. The robber bands were badly armed, but each one was united under the iron will of its leader, and carried away by his imagination. On all sides, in the huge country loosely organized for a peaceful existence, the local band scored, until it met a rival one, or its men fell out among themselves.

In the region between Moscow and Kazan, the well-to-do population fled west, away from the steadily advancing vanguard of the chief band, led by the real Pugachev. Moscow was full of refugees. Some came as far as Kursk. All men, young and old, were busy forming a militia. Anxiety was drowned in excitement. Energetic characters took the lead. Brainy suggestions sparkled on all sides.

"But you *must* have an old musket lying about somewhere; we found two in *our* lumber room," Boris, a powerfully built stocky youth with roguish brown eyes and a pink face, said eagerly. Then, catching sight of Prokhor, "Must get one for him too."

"Too young!" protested Alexis.

The boy blushed, "I'd have to know why, before I took a gun; before I did anything, for that matter."

"Why?" they laughed. "Have you been lying fast asleep on soft emerald grass or under deep blue water for the last twelve months? To kill the monster-reptile, Pugachev, of course!"

"I mean what for, not only against what."

"For the Empress, Russia, the Faith."

"Russia! They too are part of her, the Pugachevs that spring up like mushrooms. Mushrooms are part of the earth that breeds them. The Faith, yes, it is given us; but do we live by it? The Empress is beautiful and good, but very far away; hazy."

"Rubbish!" shouted Boris. Alexis looked at him sharply, ready to stand up for his younger brother. But, as he met the laughing eyes, looked at the dark smooth hair and full red lips, so like Katia's, his heart warmed and he changed his mind. Her brother must be right.

"Anyway, he's too young," he decided.

"But there's something in what he says," protested a tall thin youth with a girlish face and a bar of freckles across the bridge of his nose. And turning to Prokhor, "What is it then?"

Slowly, Prokhor crossed to the window. New thoughts were lighting up in his mind; flickering round his head; eluding him, slipping out and away. He made an effort to bring them down, right down, into his heart. With narrowing eyes, he turned round.

"They talk of freedom, yet they bring death, fire, distress. What freedom is this? Then they say they will enforce order, but you look around and see a plough abandoned in a silent field laid waste. What order is this?

"We live as in a wood torn by storms. Because of the way the wind blows, a tangle of uprooted trees piles up high on one side of us, the earth grows bare on the other. In the tangle, wild beasts hide, waiting to pounce on us, or on each other. But on the side where the wind has swept everything away, there is the tidiness of death."

"What are we to do?" asked Peter, the boy with the freckles.

"Make a fresh green path winding between the two,"

answered Prokhor joyously as though waking up. " Never leave it, and steadily make it wider. Spread it into the tangle and into the waste."

" That's it," laughed Boris. " Come on ! Come and fight for Prokhor's green path ! "

But Peter asked, " How do we make it, what of ? "

" Of freedom. A kind of tidy freedom. I can't explain. An order of a kind that doesn't kill."

" Where do we find it ? "

" I don't know." Prokhor frowned, staring at the polished floor boards.

Auntie pattered in with the keys of the lumber room. " You may go up now and look for yourselves, if you're careful ; and," turning to Alexis, " Yakov will go with you."

Prokhor soon overcame his phase of restlessness ; he had gained a new maturity. But his playfellows and his brother's friends were growing disgruntled ; and it was to him, who had overcome his despondency, that they turned when bewildered or at a loss. From them Prokhor learnt about family quarrels and the angry unhappiness of young people frustrated by their elders ; because of them, through them, he learnt the art of listening, and the delicate use of gentle, suggestive words of counsel.

When the Turks at last signed peace, and the whole of the Russian army was free to deal with Pugachev and his doubles, the excitement, that had kept all keyed up for two years, died down.

The smaller fry were quickly dealt with. Then, the Rabble Army, fiercely attacked, fled back beyond the Volga, towards the Iayik whence their leader had sprung. In the summer of 1775, Pugachev was at last captured, put in a cage, and brought to Moscow. The path of his slow progress was lined with men who had but recently accepted him as their lawful Tsar and acclaimed him as their benefactor. No abuse was too foul for him now.

In Moscow, still caged like a wild beast, he was put up in the market square to be spat on by self-righteous housewives doing their day's shopping, and to be jeered at by small boys out for fun.

Town militias were no longer needed. Yakov carried the muskets back to the lumber room. Gloomy dissatisfaction settled on the young craftsmen and tradesmen's sons of Kursk. The cup of life had gone flat, there was no head to it. Prokhor, in no mood to take part in the business—as he should by now—begged his mother and brother to let him off for a couple of months, to attend church services daily, morning and evening. The youth of Kursk often met in the Moshnins' warm study after supper. Outside, the snow was deep; the wind, keen as a knife.

"And what now?" Peter asked querulously, puckering his freckles into a mask of misery. "Every day just like the one before, and the one after. A slow walk round the store house to see if the rats have got at the grain, and if the men sit about doing nothing; then the entries into the books; then my report to my father, and the constant pretence that I think as he does; that I, too, think it important that we should cut down expenses, or raise our profits." He pursed his soft lips petulantly.

"You can't live without money," Alexis remarked. "There are the women to provide for. The children too, when you marry."

Money was getting scarce again, times were hard. He and Agatha were no longer sure they could send Prokhor to Petersburg. He might have to wait a year, or two; or even more.

"You must train yourself to examine your mind carefully," said Lukich, lighting with a shaky hand a long pipe of briar and meerschaum, the only gift of his godfather's with which he had not parted. " You must find an occupation that fits your talents. It's important. Though you may have mastered all the arguments of Plato and Aristotle, if you've not the capacity for forming a solid judgment on these matters you will not become a philosopher. So it is with commerce; so it is with everything. Prokhor's lucky: his talents and leanings are obvious and blend well."

" Perhaps we could manage it somehow, after all," thought Alexis, looking sadly at his brother who sat silent, smiling at his own thoughts.

" Yes ! " exclaimed Peter, " if I had a talent like that, if I knew I had a kind of call."

" How do you know you've not ? " asked Prokhor unexpectedly. " Russia's getting known everywhere, feared, respected. But she's not loved. How do you know you're not meant to wander about the world building churches ? Ambassadors from everywhere are coming to Petersburg now. The Empress sends hers everywhere. We're not loved because we're not properly known. We must go west, and east, and south—we must wander over the whole world—and, wherever an ambassador lives, we must build a church for him. Beautiful churches. So beautiful that all kinds of men from all over the world will come to admire them; when they see what it is we love, what we have faith in, what we hope for, they'll understand us. Then they'll love us too. Us—our country, Christ's jewel !"

Prokhor had jumped up, and was pacing the floor. Peter stared at him with eyes still dark, but where a new hope glimmered. Zakhar, a pale boy with a pointed chin, sensitive lips, and somewhat shifty little grey eyes, attentively followed Prokhor's movements; and his eyes grew more steady as they opened wider. Boris broke the spell, " Shall I chuck the hardware trade then, and go with you to build churches in China?" He and Alexis laughed, but Prokhor had started them dreaming.

Next morning, leaving church, Prokhor ran into Grisha. Together they walked to Isidor's grave.

"Thoughtful!" said the fool.

The boy, in his eagerness, ignored the irony of Grisha's tone. "As soon as the family can raise the money, I'm off, to learn; then I go abroad; to build our Russian churches there; to show the foreigners what our Church is, so that they too may learn to know and honour the Faith, our Russian Church!"

"What Russian Church?" asked Grisha in a bitter, raucous voice. Amazed Prokhor stopped. They confronted each other in silence; then, "Torn, bleeding, a house divided against itself," Grisha lamented with such sadness that Prokhor felt his heart contract. Slowly they walked on in the brilliant sunlight. Softly the dry snow crunched underfoot. Grisha spoke: "I've wandered far and wide in the land, I've measured, inch by inch, the depths of the chasm. Tsar Peter, whom they call Great, only added the finishing touch. It was his father who brought the misery; helped the proud Patriarch to excommunicate harshly, when he should have taught, explained. It was the harsh pride that did it. Mocked and persecuted, the Old Believers hardened their hopes, longings, and wrath —yes, their righteous wrath too, they hardened it into prejudice and bigotry. Millions of them. And we, who remained with Tsar and Patriarch, sharing their guilt, we lost our Patriarch pretty soon! We're given a College of German Gentlemen instead, by a Tsar, grown as German as the rest of them. A house divided against itself is no longer a house. It's a shambles."

His voice and appearance changed again, "Yes, go abroad," he hissed, his dark eyes flashing, "show it to the foreigners, show it to the Lutherans, show it to the Papists. Let them gloat on the trembling, naked, bleeding body of your Mother Church."

Prokhor, grown pale, moved his lips silently a few times. Then, " Tell me what to do, you must ! "

" Heal the wound ; heal it. Make the Body of Christ whole. Have pity. Don't show off its plight. There was enough of that on Calvary."

" How can I heal ? "

" Pray."

Time went by. The impression left by Grisha's outburst did not weaken. Prokhor asked Alexis to go slow in scraping together the money for his journey to Petersburg and his tuition there. To Agatha he said that faced by a life-long decision, he was preparing himself for it ; she understood. In the meantime, he begged her to let him take on her share of work in the business. She had grown smaller and thinner of late. And, although her limpid grey eyes still looked as steadily as before out of her face grown peaked and yellow, there were new lines of weariness about her mouth and she stooped a little, as she walked.

" I'm always tired, these days," she would say to Auntie. " Dear me," the robust old woman exclaimed. " I'll go and make you a strong cup of broth at once, dearie." Agatha sipped it dutifully, smiling a little ; it never lifted her weariness.

As spring tore in upon them, melting the deep snow into hundreds of burbling rivulets, Alexis told his family— somewhat formally requested by him to assemble in the study—that his affection for Katia had not weakened as he once thought it might. Would Agatha give him her blessing ? He was about to ask Katia's father for her hand. Did she think there was any hope ?

" But, dear," Agatha smiled, " you're a very eligible

young man, didn't you know? Katia's mother hinted as much, some time ago. And she said there would be a good dowry with the girl."

Agatha approved of Katia as a daughter-in-law but, since they were both very young, suggested that the wedding might be put off till Alexis was twenty-one. The betrothal, however, could be performed any time after Easter. And perhaps she herself had better see the parents first. Auntie had been dabbing her eyes from the outset; when all was settled she blew her nose.

By the time the spring floods had dried, the two families were seeing a great deal of each other. They formed a centre of attraction and many young people of the neighbourhood gathered round them.

Once, in the early evening, all met on a meadow outside the town gates. Mothers, aunts, and married sisters slowly walked up and down the rough path by the willows. The young people, in pairs, formed a long column down the middle of the open green expanse. They faced south. Before them, facing the same way, stood Peter. This was the popular game of *burners*, a rag-tail of the old cult of the thunder god Perun.*

Holding hands, the pairs of boys and girls chanted quickly, in unison,

> Burners burning brightly
> keep them burning brightly
> Glance on high
> small birds fly.

At the word *glance*, Peter threw his head right back. In the silken blue, two larks, all a-tremble, glittered, obliquely shone upon by the sun.

No sooner had he thrown back his head than the pair immediately behind him separated and ran forward in two wide semi-circles. As the last word of the chant died down,

* It is also a reminiscence of the ancient custom of marriage by abduction.

Peter rushed after them looking to see where they had gone. His object was to catch the girl before she and the other boy joined hands again.

But, dodging right and left, Katia was too nimble for him, so he turned round and caught hold of the boy. Though permitted, this was thought mean. Jeering at him, Katia went to the front, to be burner, while the two boys walked to the back of the column.

The next pair were Prokhor and a cousin of Katia's on a visit from Chernigov. Though she had never been to Kursk before, the girl was not shy. She was, in fact, more forthcoming than any of her cousins.

Katia threw back her head, *glancing on high*. Galeena squeezed Prokhor's hand and whispered, rising on tip-toe and bending towards him so that her hair brushed his ear.

" Make straight for the wattles over there, we'll join up behind them." She was very like Katia but prettier, taller, more fully developed. Looking down, he caught sight of a flash of white teeth between full red lips, made redder with beetroot juice; her chin and nose had been gently rubbed with the silky bark of the silver birch. Some of the fine whitish powder still clung to her skin giving it a soft bloom. He did as he was told.

Behind the wattles, yelling loud with delight and calling forth a response of cheers from the pairs on the meadow, she flung herself at him; pressed her body against his; kissed him firmly on the mouth. Then grabbing his hand looked round laughing.

" It isn't fair," shouted Katia running towards them, from behind the bushes. " This is out of bounds; we can't see you here; there must be some limit ! "

Arguing they went back. Katia, to burn once again. Prokhor and Galeena, to the back of the column.

" Why did you do that ? " he asked softly.

" I like it."

" What ? "

" Your face."

" Why ? "

" It's nice."

" It isn't ! "

She giggled, " If I say so, it must be."

At their next run, he let himself be caught by the burner, and kept away from Galeena for the rest of the evening.

All walked back together. At their gate, Prokhor and Auntie turned in, Alexis went on to see the girls home.

Agatha was in bed. The sanctuary lamp glowed like a ruby in front of the ikons in the corner. The room smelt of oil and rose water. " May I borrow your looking glass, Mama ? "

" Have you hurt yourself ? "

" No, I just want to look at something."

" Don't stay up too long."

In his room, he lighted two candles and propped up the looking glass between them. Sat down. Peered intently at his face.

Bright blue eyes. Above them wide-flung eyebrows, much darker than the long flaxen hair which, carefully parted in the middle, covered almost the whole of his ears. The eyebrows were as dark as Alexis's hair. Below the eyes, the tanned skin was stretched tight on strong cheek-bones. The nose was short, but had sensitive nostrils. The lips were broad, flat and outlined very simply, almost without curves. On the firm round chin, the skin was as taut as on the cheekbones. The down on it was changing to hair.

So this was his face. Liked, or disliked, by people. Was it him they saw when they looked at it ? Was it really him, really like him, like his real self ? Bending forward he peered into the deep blue till his head swam.

A year passed, and it was spring again. The glamour of the wedding had already faded. Katia now lived with them; yet the house, which appeared crammed before, was still just as full, but no fuller.

It was Sunday. After mass, some young neighbours gathered in the front garden. Katia handed round glasses of kvas and hot spiced buns. They sat in a row on two long benches, beside a lilac bush ready to burst into flower. The sun was warm, the breeze cool.

"When will you get down to your church building, at last?" Boris asked, passing an arm round Prokhor's shoulder.

"Don't know. It isn't the churches that really matter. It's the Church."

They looked at him. He carefully explained the situation, repeating much of what Grisha had said, and adding information picked up here and there.

"We must work for a blending of the two halves, for a healing of the wound, for a reconciliation!"

"Hush, hush, hush!" Auntie exclaimed, stopping on her way to the ice house and fluttering her podgy little white hands at him. "You'll get us all arrested, if you say such things!"

"That's it," he sighed.

When she had gone, they wanted to know more. It was up to him to find a way of doing it. They'd follow him, wherever he went; support him, whatever he did, and whatever the consequences to themselves.

Towards sunset, he sauntered over to the cemetery in search of Grisha. There he was, carefully sprinkling Isidor's grave, out of a large earthenware jar. "Just look at them," he said waving towards the pansies, "all eyes and ears. And these," bending down to the mignonette and sniffing, "the breath of angels smells like that."

"Grisha," Prokhor said, "tell me how to set about re-uniting our wounded Church? I've five followers who'll do all I tell them. What must I do?"

" Curb your pride."

" That won't help."

" Oh no, it won't," mocked Grisha, " it won't help you to attract followers, with your lips unclean. It won't help to build your ninth wonder of the world, it won't help to show off the misery of Mother Church to them who scorn her; it won't help to lead your five muts down the road of destruction: prison, banishment, death. It won't help."

" Oh don't be tiresome. Do try and understand," Prokhor exclaimed hotly. " I'm in dead earnest ! "

" And I'm in earnest too ! " thundered Grisha. " Only he may touch the sacred body, who has overcome the devil's sin (men's sins don't count). Pride brought the dark angels tumbling out of heaven. And it's there, there, at your feet; blocking the way; making a fool of you. Oh, I'm sorry, it's Grisha, the fool."

Shrugging, Prokhor turned and went home. Why wouldn't the silly old fool help when he was asked. Others were ready enough.

That night he lay awake. Taut on his back, hands clasped behind his head, he stared at the dim light of the sanctuary lamp, but saw neither it nor the dark faces of the ikons beyond. " Sorry—it's Grisha, the fool," the night mocked. " It's Prokhor, the fool," he almost moaned aloud, passing in review the whole of his life.

A pampered baby, a boy easily and always getting his way, a lad for whose brilliant future Alexis was ready to plod stolidly, cutting down the expenses of the rest of the family. Idolized by his boy friends, admired by the girls, treated as an equal by the learned Lukich. Through the whole of this life, the glossy coils of the snake of pride crept, surreptitiously keeping out of sight. But the moment Grisha pricked the reptile, it rose on its tail, in all its vile splendour and hissed, revealing its nature.

He slept, in the end, but woke almost at once. It was very early. Dressing quickly, he went straight to the cemetery. There was no one about. In the gentle sunlight birds sang, chirped, twittered, exchanged their mating calls.

Clasping his knees, Grisha sat on a child's tombstone. His head was thrown back, and he was singing a heart-rending melody, in an incredibly high voice.

Humbly, yet resolutely, Prokhor went up to him. Grisha continued to sing,

" On a sunlit hill in Jerusalem they hoisted up my Love
In a Russian wood in the dead of night I finished off the job
Woe's me ! "

Prokhor walked round and placed himself between Grisha and the sun. The head of his shadow rested on Grisha's knees. The fool repeated the refrain three times. When at last his soaring song ceased, Prokhor's low " Forgive me," fell like an offering at his feet.

Without changing his position, still gazing up into the sky, Grisha drawled, in a sing-song, " The voice that issues from the meeting point of the six wings proclaims : Pride blocks man's way. Let him grind his way through the block with the tool of obedience." Then, standing up, stretching himself and yawning, he went on very simply, " Pakhomius, Abbot of Sarov, was a big boy here in Kursk, when I was small. He was kind to my foster mother when her house was burnt. It has its martyrs, Sarov : Forty years ago, Abbot Efrem, accused of high treason—he loved Mother Church—was dragged to Petersburg, kept in prison there for three years ; died of it. Father John too. Him I knew. High treason again. Defrocked. Imprisoned in the fortress of Orenburg for sixteen years. Yes, the worst of us always torment the best, and mock those whom we ourselves cut off. And all the while, right in our midst, heathen villages live on here, there, everywhere, untaught, un-redeemed, the blackest of our sins."

"Sarov!" said Prokhor dreamily, "One of Auntie's brothers was a monk there. He died young. Torn by wolves when walking back alone, through the woods, one winter night."

"Yes, the Temniki is a great thick forest; and wild. Obedience is a tussle with death there."

For the rest of that day, Prokhor's mind was not on his work. He had been drifting blindly. Now the scales had fallen from his eyes. He saw himself and his life's aim clearly. In the quiet centre of his heart, below the excitement of dreams, he had steadily longed only for the joy of contemplation. In his mind, too, above all desire for knowledge, he had thirsted for the certitude of contemplation. But he had feared obedience, shied away from its disturbing depths. He feared obedience no longer now. Hankered after it. He'd go to Sarov and devote himself to it there.

Pride again. He'd go! Who was he to decide where to seek it? The country was full of monasteries. And since this was the one he longed to go to, he'd put the choice in the hands of another.

That evening he joined Agatha as she sat over her embroidery in the garden, and told her of his newly discovered old desire. "I know," she said looking up, her steady eyes large in her pale face, "I've always known you would. Where will you go?"

"Where should I go?"

She sat silent; as though listening intently to the trills of a nightingale hidden away in the lilac bush. It might have been the lilac singing.

Then said, "Why not go to Kiev? Old Dosifei lives in one of the Lavra anchorholds there. He has the sight. Ask him."

Alexis, Auntie, Katia, Niusha, Yakov, and Lukich accepted Prokhor's decision calmly, though some were astonished while others were not. Peter, Zakhar, and Boris asked their parents to let them go with him. Two other young neighbours wished to join in the pilgrimage, and on July 4, 1776, the six boys set out to cover on foot the two hundred and fifty miles to Kiev.

Before starting, the pilgrims asked for their parents' blessing. Prokhor took Agatha's on his knees; then he prostrated himself and touched the ground at her feet with his forehead. When he rose, she hung round his neck a very old crucifix wrought in brass. There were tears of tenderness—not of sorrow—in her eyes. Auntie wept loudly.

Staff in hand, small bundles on their backs, they left Kursk early in the morning. Singing psalms, in a mood of elated companionship, they swung past orchards and through fields where heavy corn swayed in the wind. They slept in the open, by hay ricks, or in the barns of friendly peasants, who sometimes gave them a bowl of gruel, or bread to take with them. Their feet sank ankle deep in the fine dust of the road. They drank spring water when they could get it, and carried no bottles.

On their arrival in Kiev, Prokhor's companions settled down in the Lavra guest-house while he pushed on, alone, to a secluded glade, seven miles off, where Dosifei now lived. Coming out from behind the trees at last, he knelt to greet the *starets*. Dosifei ran forward, raised the boy, led him to a large trunk that lay nearby, sat down beside him and—smiling with all his wrinkles, blinking his shortsighted eyes—prepared to listen.

When Prokhor had finished the story of his life, he looked up at his host, "I've heard the call; I know my way—obedience. But where shall I seek this? That, I've come to ask."

Dosifei munched his crinkled lips with toothless gums.

Birds chirped, trees rustled, butterflies flitted past.

Then, sighing deeply, " Go home," he said, " live in obedience to the whole of your family. Humble your mind till your heart burns and rings with the Jesus prayer. Pray constantly."

Prokhor looked at him blankly. Dosifei rose. A little man, his white head—with a bald patch in the middle—reached no higher than Prokhor's shoulder.

Lifting his hand to give the boy a blessing, he added, " In two years' time you'll be ready for Sarov. May your life begin and end there. I'll pray."

Prokhor bent down and, with tender reverence, kissed the old man's hand.

THE PLACE

LATE in the thirteenth century, the occupying forces of the Tartar horde set about to fortify strong points in the conquered land of the Rūs. While easy in the steppe country, this was difficult further north, where thick forest stretches for thousands of miles.

After weeks of slow progress, one band of Asiatics at last came to a high, wooded hill, situated in the heart of the forest of Temniki and encircled by two rivers. Nimbly the shaggy little mounts swam the rivers and scaled the precipitous banks of sandstone. Then the men and their women threw up walls of earth, pitched their tents and settled down, praising the sagacity of their leader. They called the place Saraklych and stayed on it for a hundred years; sons, born on the spot, took over from ageing fathers. Saraklych was an advanced outpost. Saraklych meant men of cruel courage; and they were practical, unhampered by sentiment or by a moral code.

From time to time the Saraklych went on raiding expeditions in search of more horses and more women; their population was growing fast. Whenever a protesting local priest ventured to visit them in their lair, striving to reason with them or hoping to touch their hearts, the comic creature was made the laughing stock of the robust, ribald tribe; the entertainment over, he was given a martyr's death.

At the close of the fourteenth century, the great tide of invading Mongols receded east; the evacuated stronghold became the haunt of marauding robbers and dangerous criminals. For three hundred years trappers and gatherers of wild honey avoided the neighbourhood; no villager came that way of his free will. Gradually, its name was shortened to Sarov.

The first anchorité to settle there, came upon it by chance, at a time when the hill stood unoccupied. Presently, other solitaries joined him, though they lived separately, each man in his own cave. But soon, they were all driven out by a large robber band. After this, hermits and criminals succeeded each other in waves.

Slowly, persistently a rumour began to spread: from time to time, on the big days of the Christian calendar, a light was seen to hover over the hill; the air above, rang with peals of many bells.

A villager or two, greedy by nature and still clinging to the old pre-Christian superstitions, secretly repaired thither with spade and pick. The light and bells, they thought, were a true showing: a great hoard of riches must lie buried there.

They dug long and, at last, unearthed a bronze tryptich and three large crosses of rough-hewn stone; the tryptich had a Presentation delicately wrought on its inner surface. Disgusted, the men left the things where they had found them, gathered their tools, and went home.

The crosses and tryptich were found lying about the hill by the hermit Izaac who, in the beginning of the eighteenth century finally settled there. In 1705, Prince Kugushev, the owner of the forest land made Izaac a present of the hill and of two rivers, Satis and Sarovka, where their source touches it. In the spring of the next year, Izaac laid the foundation stone of a wooden church dedicated to Our Lady of the Holy Well. Proud men treading the hard path of obedience, gathered round him.

Prokhor started on his way to Sarov in the autumn of 1778. Of the five young men who had accompanied him to Kiev, Peter and Zakhar were with him again. Paul and Ivan already lived at Sarov, going through their novitiate; Boris, at the last moment, decided to stay at home.

Prokhor's two years of obedience to his family had passed smoothly. Too smoothly, perhaps. Since he was careful never to express a wish, Auntie, Alexis, and even Agatha deployed much ingenuity to guess what this might be at any given moment. He lived as on a high mountain, in rarified air. His family watched over him and, plodding at the foot of the mountain, protected him from life's crudities. During the whole of these two years he had received only two jolts; Lukich was the cause of both.

The winter after the Kiev visit was unusually hard. When Alexis once mentioned that Lukich was apparently having "unpleasantness" with his superiors at the government office and might be sacked, Agatha suggested they should offer him some of their fire logs; these would at least keep his rooms warm. Early next morning, Prokhor set out on his mother's errand. The landlady informed him icily that Lukich now lived in a room over the drinking-house. Dismayed, Prokhor hurried there.

A broad faced, snub nosed scullery boy lazily swept the floor. Without stopping his song, he answered Prokhor's enquiry by pointing with his thumb up a rickety staircase. Then shouted after him, " Last on the left."

It was a crooked door, partly torn off its hinges. Prokhor barely touched it, and it flew open with a creak, loud and long. Lukich, in an old dressing gown, his greying hair in a tousled mat, stared from the bed where he lay under a rug and overcoat. " Alex-no-Prokh ! " he mumbled blinking his bleary eyes. " Sit. Listen." With jerky vehemence, he pulled Prokhor down on to a stool by the bed. " He shouldn't have dedicated it to the Princess, a nineteen-year old-daughter of a king, pah ! Silly, silly, silly. Think of it : ' Those who are familiar with mathematics cannot comprehend metaphysics,' he wrote, Descartes did, ' while those conversant with metaphysics cannot understand mathematics. The *only* mind (the peeved voice rose to a squeak) the only mind to which both alike are easy is yours ! ' Hers (with a whimper) ' And so I am compelled to regard it as incomparable. It is high-minded wisdom that I reverence in you ! ' Hers, in her. It should have been me. The Principles of Philosophy should have been dedicated to Ivan Lukich ! "

Agitated, he searched among the folds of the rug, in the pockets of his overcoat, under the pillow. " There, there, look for it there," he pointed to a small chest that stood open on the floor, and into which his clothes and periwig had been flung, " No, no, no, here," and he extracted his snuff box from under his back. Scrabbled in it with an unsteady finger. Empty. He raised to his mouth the long pipe that had lain on the floor within reach, sucked at it. Empty too. Not worth lighting.

" He was in no condition to listen to reason, could take in nothing," Prokhor told Agatha later. " What shall we do ? "

Agatha and Auntie went round in the afternoon. Lukich refused to move or be moved, wanted to stay where he was, as he was, liked it, wished to be left alone. Alexis was equally unsuccessful.

It was at this time that news of Dosifei's death reached Kursk. Prokhor grew even more assiduous at church services and more meticulous in carrying out the rule of preparation that Dosifei had given him to follow at home. The rest of his time he entirely devoted to the discipline of the Jesus Prayer—the prayer of the publican, repeated many hundred times a day—and to reading the Bible and the Fathers.

When, months later, Prokhor once again thought of calling at the room over the drinking-house, he met the scullery boy running down the rickety stairs. " Gawn," the boy answered Prokhor's enquiry. " Where to ? " The boy shrugged his shoulders up to his ears, and sprinted out of sight as quick as a mouse : the proprietress was calling. She knew no more than the boy.

Prokhor was perturbed. Lukich could not have died ; people would have known if he had. But where could he be ? How did he keep alive ? All the family enquired everywhere. No one knew.

A few days later, Prokhor, on his way back from church, ran into Grisha, ambling along hurriedly, a load of faggots and logs on his back, a loaf of bread and a bag of buck-wheat in his hands.

" Come," he grunted.

" Where to ? "

" The Lector's given me a room. The old larder, built on to his porch. He's put a stove in, good man."

Prokhor carried the bag and loaf. In the porch Grisha cautioned him, " Don't speak, he's busy."

Lukich, in a nondescript garment, obviously discarded by a smaller and plumper man, his grey hair parted in the middle, and smoothed down on both sides of his yellow face—with its purple little nose burning in the middle of it—carefully moved about the small room, duster in hand. Silently he took the faggots and logs, and made up the fire. His eyes were clear though blind to everything but the job in hand. His lips moved all the time. Grisha was training him in inner prayer.

The fool turned to Prokhor: " Tell Agatha, we could do with fire logs, buck-wheat and the like. He cooks."

When Prokhor went to say good-bye to them before leaving for Sarov, Lukich, his nose hardly more pink than the rest of his face, had just got back from the church warden of St. Sergius; he had been offered the job of choir master. Elated, he enlarged on all the innovations and embellishments he would now introduce into their bare room; Grisha need never beg again. " Rust and dust, rust and dust," the fool went about muttering irritably.

Demure, tidy, his periwig carefully adjusted, Lukich was there again when Prokhor left his own home. At Agatha's only sign of weakness, " I hoped you'd stay till I was dead, then go," Lukich hurried to her side.

Obedience, Prokhor remembered. " Shall I ? " he asked, his heart missing a beat.

" No, you must go," she hurried to assure him. *Let it be, woman, it is no longer yours to hold*, she remembered.

" Quite sure ? "

" Yes. Quite. Go. I want you to." She clutched Lukich by the hand and leant against his shoulder.

It took the three boys well over a month to walk to Sarov from Kursk. Since it was late autumn, they slept in any shelter they happened to be passing at night fall: overcrowded peasant huts; tradesmen's dewllings, small and cosy; opulent houses of prosperous merchants; luxurious manors of the landed gentry.

October darkened into November, then November hardened into December. Rain poured down more steadily, and the angry wind howled more often ; roads changed into bogs ; grey crows cawed over black fields ; bare trees creaked sadly. Then the snow came ; it muffled all objects in soft white shawls but made the least sound, even the most distant, ring near and clear.

Through the changing landscape, the three boys plodded on, sometimes singing psalms, at others keeping silent. They got to Sarov late, one still, moonlit night ; it was the eve of the Presentation.

Abbot Pakhomuis, overjoyed at the arrival of his young townsmen, received them warmly. He and Isidor had been boys together. Prokhor was at once put by him under obedience to the cellarer ; " A man of sweetest wisdom," Pakhomius said.

But Prokhor, coming into Joseph's cell after half an hour's quiet talk with the dignified, gentle, grey-haired abbot, felt a twinge of misgiving. Small and fiery, with long raven black beard and hair, and with beetling eyebrows, the cellarer looked forbidding. Then he smiled, disclosing a huge mouth with a few large yellow teeth scattered in it here and there. This shabby smile lighted up his face with an expression of such tender compassion that Prokhor at once knew no other man could guide him as wisely as Joseph would. From that day, through all the eight years of his noviciate, he waited on Joseph and tidied his cell.

Though gradual, his initiation into the life was thorough. Tall, broad in the shoulders and very strong, he at once joined one of the timber gangs in the forest. Lumbering was the communal work at Sarov. Between church services and their diverse charges, novices and monks felled the mighty trees and piled their great trunks on the river banks. They would be floated downstream when the spring floods were over. All day the still, frosty air rang with the song of metal hitting wood, and the soft swish of sleds, skimming over snow.

Conversation was not forbidden during communal work. More often than not, the novices—mostly young men and rough—indulged in it above measure. A chance allusion led to an intentional one, and presently, every sentence, innocent enough to one who might be passing by, was smeared over with a sticky bloom of obscenity. The older monks, having been novices themselves, could not fail to know of this, yet they did nothing about it.

When Prokhor refused to take part in the banter and chat, he made himself unpopular. When, appalled, he strove to keep his mind busy with prayer, he failed pitiably and found himself automatically repeating one sequence of words, while he listened with hostile avidity to the other.

Joseph's comment on this he found disheartening: " Their words are their concern : steady your own mind." " But they stop my praying." " No one can do that. If you can't keep your mind centred on inner work, leave it. If you must listen, do so frankly. There's no need for you to pray at communal work."

After a few weeks of this, Prokhor came to despair of novices and monks alike. Was this what he had sought and longed for ? He found relief only in church. There, standing with downcast eyes and always on the same place, he steeped himself in the service, striving to penetrate the entire liturgical pattern, and the whole of its significance of thought and experience ; striving to become the ground where the sequence of liturgical thought and the succession of liturgical experience are joined.

But he could not spend all his time there. Joseph, who often varied his charges, made him baker, carpenter, watchman, and sacristan in turns. Soon, even the presence of the older monks, in the carpenter's shop and in the bakery, disturbed him and deflected his attention from prayer. He came to despair of himself.

Dispirited, disgusted with everyone and everything,

he sought the solitude of his cell. Tensely, he stood in front of the lectern; one of the books he had been provided with lay open before him. He toiled hard, striving to penetrate to the innermost core of the words, and to memorise them.

But his mind was dull, his soul empty. Pictures of his childhood rose before his mind's eye. Exasperated, he tossed his head; noticed some books lying about untidily: left the lectern to put them away; the name "Dosifei" caught his eye. The visit to Kiev! What a man, what a guide, what a monk. Friendliness, wisdom, understanding. Blinking eyes, bald patch, fluttering birds. "Get ready for Sarov. May your life begin and end there!"

Groaning he dragged himself back to his reading. *And Esther spake yet again before the king, and fell down at his feet and besought him with tears.* Was he not beseeching his King with tears too? Why, then, did his King countenance such defiling of his humble servant? How could he permit these men light-heartedly to insult his servant's soul?

Blind hands gladly write obscene words on a simple white wall; for no better reason than men's secret urge to leave some mark, expressive of themselves, on the provocative simplicity of a surface too smooth, too white, too simple to be tolerated; too alluring not to be defiled. When night comes—the night of the year—with all the hopelessness of autumn rains; while night reigns throughout the hardening bitterness of winter frosts; when night is shattered in the uncompromising roar and glare of the pitiless thaw; the sullied wall, rained upon, frozen and thawed, imperceptibly and yet irrevocably ceases to be. Crumbling to dust, it gives up its secrets, imprints them on the shroud of the great void. Branded, Prokhor's sullied soul will live on, a body of shame. Branded by the froth of other men's slovenly hilarity, it will live on, eternally unclean. They do not even understand what they are doing

—blind hands. Whose then is the sight? Whose the sight and driving will?

The cumulative effect of their daily persiflage—their daily affront of the temple of the spirit—had torn a deep cleft between him and the men around him. He was alone; so lonely; and yet not alone: Beyond the immediate, isolating void that enclosed him, a crowd of monks and novices grinned and mocked. Lean or fat, tall or short, jovial or cynical, old or young, they crowded round, mouthing words, and sequences of words. The wounds they dealt would heal; time would heal them. But what in heaven or earth could remove the cicatrice of sullying insults? What? Who?

And Esther spake yet again before the King, and fell down at his feet and besought him with tears. Did Galeena ever cry? Had anyone seen her eyes fill with tears, her full lips tremble? What was she doing now? Staying with Katia, perhaps.

And he, what was he doing here, where no one understood him, or cared for him? He had advanced quickly at home. Why had he forfeited the warmth of human companionship? Only to lose the impetus that had driven him along.

Empty and restless, he sought Peter in the infirmary. A loud, hollow cough resounded down the long passage. "They're transferring me to the Kiev Lavra as soon as I'm better," Peter said. "I'll never get rid of this here."

"How lonely I'll be. Could I go too?"

"But you're so strong, just look at you! And it's you who wanted to come.'

"Dosifei," thought Prokhor. "*Live and die there!*"

"Zakhar's getting on fine," Peter added casually.

That Prokhor knew. On the way to the infirmary he had met Zakhar hurrying on some errand of Father Isaiah's. He was popular; cracked the best jokes with the othre novices, his little grey eyes twinkling mischievously all the while. His brown hair, fluffy and fine like a baby's, delicately framed his pale face, broad at the cheekbones, pointed at the chin; his air of innocence added piquancy to the crude undercurrent of his words. Yet, the older monks praised him for his quick wits and constant cheerfulness. He was popular indeed, and had completely forgotten that he once looked up to Prokhor, and had sought his company and advice. The place was getting him down too, in another way. Prokhor despaired of the whole of Sarov. Perhaps it was a mistake to have come? The urge an illusion, the longing a temptation.

When he wanted to cut down his sleep and food, Joseph forbade it, insisting that he must sleep four hours at least —from nine till one in the morning—and eat a good meal at midday and a light one for supper. Left to himself, Prokhor would have starved, and prayed all night.

Gradually he came to have frequent headaches; they increased his irritation with all around him, made concentration more difficult, and his misery more acute.

Unbearably lonely, he longed for companionship. But not for any that could be had; only for the unrealizable: Dosifei, Agatha, Alexis, Auntie, Lukich, Grisha. Galeena? Should he have trained to be an architect after all? A great architect; and had a family of his own. None of that was incompatible with a Christian life, more Christian than this, surely.

In his agony he sought complete solitude. Pakhomius allowed him to spend some of his free time in the forest now. The summer had come; Peter had left; Zakhar was away begging; the other two boys who had come with him were transferred to monasteries in the far north.

Prokhor put up a tent of green branches at half an hour's quick walk from the banks of the Satis. As months slipped by, the whole of his active life except the hours spent in the forest, became a distasteful serfdom. Only here did he find himself. Secluded in his green tent, he trained his heart in a new attentiveness to inner prayer and toiled to cleanse his mind of all that blocks the sight, all that blinds the eye of the mind.

At last Joseph let him cut out the evening meal, and eat nothing on Fridays and Wednesdays. Prokhor set himself to uproot covetousness in the most primitive sphere of human life. Gradually, his spirit became free of the shackles of the lower soul. But the dark soul hit back as discarded shackles will.

When the winter grew colder, his body began to swell. Painfully, he moved about his duties, then was forced to stay in bed. He lay in his cell for more than a year, unconscious at times, and in constant pain. Pakhomius and Joseph nursed him in turns, waiting on him as novices wait on older monks. His illness grew worse.

Faces, familiar of old, swam round him in a haze. As they receded, the pattern of the lives that they evoked, appeared before him clearly, picked out in threads of light on a background, the colour of the great void. He came nearer to understanding the mysteries which are expressed in physical forms and in the pattern of lives.

Auntie's bulky body, pressed out as it were by her affection which streamed towards those who lived near her, was never checked, in its actions, by her precise and quick little mind, adequate for dealing with small and immediate matters but incapable of coping with large problems and ultimate issues. These she ignored, preferring to devote her attention and imagination to the needs of the people she loved. Her concern with the welfare of others was her constant, though unconscious, spiritual exercise. Endowed with wisdom of the heart, she understood men and human situations which remained impenetrable to minds more developed than hers but dry, lacking in sympathy.

Agatha, consumed by the effort to find a balance between wisdom and intelligence, between affection and reserve, carried a woman's burden in the home and a man's burden in the family business. She performed her double task with silent courage, and was slowly breaking under the burden; but her spirit was strong, and she bore the destruction of her body with quiet, matter-of-fact pluck.

Alexis, loyal and reliable, was ambitious for his family and his friends, but humble in his estimate of himself. He had found his niche early and had never strayed from it; kept it and himself meticulously tidy, and would grow to the stature it permitted, omitting nothing required to do so.

Gradually Prokhor became familiar with the essential significance of these and other lives. Then he attained to a foretaste of an even greater, all embracing pattern of life; the universal life of the whole of creation.

Lukich had often dwelt on the endless fight of freedom and order. Whenever exaggerated, he said, they hardened: freedom to so complete a disregard of others that it caused a man to drop out of the corporate life of human kind; order—to the clamping down, to the stifling of every spontaneous creative effort and every free thought, to the crippling of the spirit of man.

Grisha, free and untidy, had brought order into the life of the meticulously tidy Lukich, grown disorderly. Agatha, Alexis, Auntie had nursed his own freedom. Sarov restricted him till he hardly knew how to breathe. Yet through that restriction, through the misery of it, he had come to another freedom. Life's inscrutable secrets were slowly shedding their veils. The interlocking of lives was becoming apparent.

The wings of his soul, folded round his spirit, stirred and slowly opened on to the timeless. Obedient to the call, fearless of consequences, he was pierced by a ray of life. Concrete physical events resulted from his spiritual awakening.

Later, the whole incident was interpreted in the idiom best understood by the Russian peasant : a short-hand of verbal oleographs used to record spiritual facts and achievements which it veils. The naïve Russian Christian accepts the oleographs as they stand ; those who are less naïve, penetrate to their symbolism ; the least naïve understand the spiritual reality beyond ; the unbelieving reject the whole occurrence.

The tradition records : " Slowly, silently, the door of Serafim's cell opened ; St. Mary, the obedient handmaiden—accompanied by the apostles Peter and John— entered, dressed as a wayfarer. She said, ' We must ease the pain of our steadfast obedientiary. For the love of Christ I ease it.' Resting her left hand on his forehead, she raised her right one, and pierced his side with her staff. The water that flowed out through the pierced skin on his side, drained his body dry."

Soon Prokhor was able to get up. But while he was still prostrate with weakness, his hair came off, like a wig. When it grew again, it was white as snow.

Catherine II was enforcing her German ideas of tidiness and order on the whole of the Russian land. Misery increased everywhere. Pakhomius suggested that a wing of one of the Sarov buildings should be converted into a hospital for incurables and the senile. The monks agreed, and decided to build, over the cell where Prokhor had lain ill, a church for the hospital. The boy asked to be one of the novices sent to collect donations.

Late on a bleak night in January he came to Kursk, and knocked at his mother's door. They had not expected him. As he stood in the entrance, tall, gaunt, his large cornflower-blue eyes bright in his yellow face—dark, under the shock of white hair, as the face of an ikon—the rejoicing of his family was tearful.

Katia hurried him upstairs to look at little Prokhor, a

few weeks old. " How tiny," he murmured. " But so like you, so joyous," she whispered proudly, looking up with a smile. Then her eyes wavered and, honestly, she added, "As you were before. He's really more like his father now."

Alexis was putting on weight. His face had acquired the chubbiness of an honest, comfortable, contented burgher. His hair had grown a little darker, and his eyes were losing their dreamy look. Since times were hard and the business was not to have an architect of its own, he had dropped, with a sigh but without a qualm, the ambitions of the last twenty years. *Moshnin's* reverted to the humble, unassuming merchant builder's shop it had been in the life-time of Isidor's father. Romance had died out of it, but it remained an honest and reliable firm.

In Agatha's room, Prokhor knelt by her bed; she had not left it for many months. " God has granted my prayer," she smiled, " my carnal eyes have rested on you once again." He kissed her hand, small, dry, with no flesh between the ivory skin and the fine bones.

Next day they told him of Lukich. His success with the St. Sergius choir was such, that the Old Countess had got him to spend three days a week at Lipovo, the biggest country house in the district. He gave music lessons to her three grand-daughters and was ordered to train the village choir to outshine St. Sergius's by next Christmas. The Countess, who drank deep of the heady cup proffered by the Hyperborean Rosicrucians, had set her heart on this success for reasons too vague and too involved to be expressed clearly. But she felt the need of it all the more deeply for that.

The moment he got back from Lipovo, Lukich learnt of Prokhor's presence in the town. It was late on a frosty evening, and he, dog tired; but taking all the money he had been given that day, wrapping it in a sheet of clean white paper, and writing a touching dedication on it, he at once set off to Agatha's.

The fitful wind heaped huge piles of snow in one place, and disclosed bald patches of smooth ice in another. High up in the distant dark sky, stippled with twinkling stars, the moon moved in and out of fleet clouds. Where they touched her, she painted them a tender pink. A little further away, they were pale green ; beyond that, dull grey.

He had never seen her so bright, the moon; never felt such a warm, intimate interest in her. What could it be ? Surely the first glimmer of an intuition, as the Countess would say. All his life he had waited and longed for one. Here it was at last ; the foretaste and unshatterable knowledge of a great truth. The crowning event of his life. The event that brought all its scraps into a glorious oneness. By the morrow, this exhilarating, feverish comprehension of a truth, that lay hidden below the semblance of things, would have cooled down. Then he would carefully build up the deductive reasoning. This would lead any dunce to the very heart of his intuitive perception.

He laughed, amazed that none should have thought of it before : the other side of the moon, her perpetually hidden side, reflects into the space beyond her the spiritual achievements of man. The immortal spirits of the ether, those who eternally live in the fourth, the highest sphere, drink them up out of the orbit of the moon—the huge celestial goblet. The spiritual achievements of man are sucked up by the nether, shining, side of the moon—a tide as it were ; a sort of tide. What a discovery ! He'd tell the Countess tomorrow ; she'd understand.

Laughing, he waved his long, bony hand to the orb that had inspired him. The wind blew more fiercely but he was almost there, and ran forward, blowing the moon a kiss. Responding, she rushed down towards him, all her stars tumbling round her ; dancing wildly they sang snatches out of the harmony of the spheres; then, she enshrouded him in sparkling white.

Inadvertently leaving the snow path, he had taken his last hurried steps on a long stretch of ice; slipped and overbalanced backward; from the great height of his long body he crashed his head against the metal-hard surface, and fractured his skull. Coma quickly changed to death. Early in the morning the yard-servants found him frozen stiff. Kursk was shattered. All clubbed together to give the Original, whom they had come to love, the most splendid funeral. The Countess said it was all profoundly symbolical.

On their return from the cemetery, Auntie, Katia, and Prokhor gathered in the study for a few minutes, before returning to their occupations. Sitting in a corner of the divan, Auntie dabbed her eyes. "Poor, poor Lukich. I loved him. Like a son. More perhaps." "Auntie!" exclaimed Katia, "at your age!" "What of it? It's our brain that dries up, or softens, or whatever it is. The heart's always young." Holding her handkerchief to her face, she rose to go to her room. But when Prokhor caught her in his arms, and patted her soothingly on her cushiony shoulder blades, she fitted her face comfortably between his arm and chest, and wept aloud; inconsolably; with open mouth, like a child.

Prokhor had collected all the money he could hope for in Kursk. On the last day he called at the Lector's for a sum that had been promised him. "He's gone, Grisha has," sadly bewildered, the kindly old man looked round the room. It had the air of desolation usual to dogs and rooms that have lost their master. "Oh no!" Prokhor protested. Until that day he could find no opportunity for a talk with his friend. And now, "But yes," the Lector insisted, "he'd been making bast clogs for the last eighteen months. Seemed to have settled down. We thought he'd be here for life. Now, the wind alone can find him!"

The brothers spent their last few minutes together alone in the study. " Don't let your soul kill off your body too soon," Alexis smiled shyly. " Oh no," Prokhor said. " When you hear of my death, you'll follow. Not till little Prokhor's eldest child thinks of marrying though." Alexis looked at him curiously. In the porch he bowed low to the departing guest.

Back at Sarov, Prokhor was set the task of making the " throne,"* for the hospital church. After carefully choosing seasoned cypress wood, he worked at it with sustained zest. As he worked, he pondered on the shape life was taking outside the monastery walls, and on the changing content of his own thoughts and feelings.

When news of Agatha's death reached him, it was no news but a final confirmation of what he had learnt on his visit home. He prayed for her no more and no less than before; only named her in another part of his prayers; placed her name by the side of Isidor, Dosifei, and Lukich.

Again he came to hanker after solitude. But the monks insisted that he should pull his weight in the communal work and carry his share of charges. And Pakhomius said, " Your evil will must be curbed. Man's feeble spark of good will cannot prevail unaided. Your own reason would find some wily excuse, and circumvent the curbing. Only their reason, unreasonable though it be, can curb your evil will. You must penetrate the whole mystery of obedience." Groaning inwardly, Prokhor complied with his superior's instructions.

At last, on a bright spring day ringing with running water and the song of birds, Prokhor was professed and given the name of Serafim, suggested by the abbot and approved by the monks. But the pattern of his daily life did not change perceptibly till he was ordained deacon in October of the same year, 1786.

* The Altar is called Throne in Russian.

During the whole six years and ten months of his diaconate, Serafim served Pakhomius and Joseph when either of them officiated. If this happened to be on a Sunday or on one of the feast-days, he kept vigil in church for the whole of the previous night. At mass he felt the sweetness of the Presence in a new, more concrete, manner. Sometimes he saw Its heralds in the form which his education and background suggested to him : they came and went as streaks of lightning, blinding bright; but between their coming and their going, they paused by the altar, as winged youths robed in gold and white.

The monks still muttered and grumbled whenever he talked of seeking solitude, but Pakhomius permitted him to choose a site, some four miles away from Sarov, and to build a hermit's hut there.

The abbot was growing frail. Tall and thin, he was beginning to stoop, and his dark grey eyes looked sadly out of his thin face that had acquired the quality of Chinese ivory. Now he never left the monastery walls without taking Serafim with him. On long drives through the country they mostly discussed the problems of souls that seek guidance.

Once, business took them to the neighbourhood of the nunnery of Divei. The rich landowner of the district, who heard of it, asked them to stay at his house. His son, full of news, had just arrived from Petersburg, and the two monks heard a vivid description of the events in Paris, of the French King's flight, arrest, and execution.

"And now," said the landowner's son, lazily lolling back in his chair and addressing his father, " that brave country has conquered the Austrian Netherlands, is threatening Holland, has torn up the Treaty of the Scheldt, is inciting the Irish and others to rebellion ; she'll be Queen of the World soon."

" The eternal, evil war between man's determination to

seek freedom for himself, and his desire to keep others in rigid order under his sway," sighed Serafim.

"Indeed?" their young host stopped the flow of his eloquence to stare through narrowed eyelids at the young monk:

"Only in the monk's cell is that frightful fight even more bitter," Pakhomius mused aloud.

The young host transferred his supercilious stare from the young monk to the old one.

"Can Pakhomius really mean that?" Serafim wondered.

They arrived at Divey during the last hours of the foundress Alexandra. The dying woman dragged herself back to life. Begged Pakhomius not to leave her nuns, to stand by them always. Drifted away, overpowered by death. With a supreme act of will, came back once more.

"Promise, Abbot, promise," she insisted hoarsely, gasping for breath.

Pakhomius bent over her, "Peace, Mother. I promise and (pointing to Serafim) he will care for them when I follow you."

She turned her glazing eyes on Serafim. An incipient smile lifted the corners of her mouth. She closed her eyes. When, after the requiem service, they took leave of the body, the waxen face was still smiling.

Russia is a country of extremes in all things. Years of abundance and years of famine constantly succeed each other. Towards the end of Serafim's diaconate, the governments of Penza, Tambov, and Ryazan were particularly hard hit. Pakhomius ordered the emergency barns to be flung open. For seven months, Sarov supplied grain to the famished population of the immediate neighbourhood. When the stocks were almost exhausted, the monks, fearing the agony of death by hunger, began to mutter. The monastery was like a ship on the eve of a mutiny. The abbot assembled all his men and spoke to them on compassion—the human link between good and evil.

" Does any one of us wish to outlive our brothers ? If so, let him stand before us and say why. Of what avail is a life, preserved at the cost of another's death ? No, we shall give away all, to the last bushel. Pray that our barns may be replenished, and prepare yourselves for death. What greater joy is there for a sinner than to die combating the death of his neighbour ? "

Some left the abbot elated, burning with a steady flame of exaltation ; others slunk away, shamefaced.

Wagon loads of grain came pouring in, sent to Pakhomius from distant parts, where the crop had been abundant that year. One morning, digging up new ground for a kitchen garden, Serafim hit on a slab of stone. He removed it and found the entrance to a large stone room filled with grain. Neither the monks nor the villagers were to perish of hunger that year.

Though Pakhomius was getting very old and weak, he took the thanksgiving service. Serafim served him as usual but, when he came out of the altar* to give his blessing to the people and monks, all humbly kneeling, he suddenly stopped as though transfixed : he had perceived the Presence, and was touched by it. The tradition records : " A beam of light, unseen by others, shot in at the entrance and, piercing the entire length of the dark church, rested its end on his heart. Surrounded by a host of angels, the Son of Man advanced down the narrow path of gold, blessing the kneeling congregation."

Thinking Serafim must have been taken ill, two other deacons hurriedly came up to him and led him back into the altar, beyond the ikonostasis, where the crowd could not see him. He stood there long, rooted to the ground.

* The eastern end of an Orthodox church is separated from the nave by a high partition called *ikonostasis*. The whole of the building beyond the partition is called "the Altar."

Gentle heat made his cheeks glow, a sweetness never before experienced brought a smile to his lips. When mass was over, he burst into song.

Later, Pakhomius and Joseph stopped him on his way into the forest. " What was it that ailed you ? " they asked. He told them. Joseph turned away, as though engrossed in the fight of two sparrows, but listened carefully for a sign of hesitation, a trace of self-consciousness. He could detect none.

Pakhomius said, " When we were boys together, your father and I, we bathed all summer in a small clear stream. If a bubble formed on the surface of the water, it would cast a curious shadow on the river bed of fine clean sand. This shadow, very dark, had an intolerably luminous border right round it in the white sand." He put out his hand and rested it on Serafim's shoulder. " You've touched the edge of the bright circle ; get ready to fight the darkness inside."

Presently, in his talks with the older monks, Pakhomius suggested that Serafim should be allowed to seek the solitude he longed for. The sickness of his first years in the monastery had never returned in full force but his legs were swelling again, and the sores on them would not heal. No longer physically fit to carry on the work that the monks exacted of him, he should not be kept at it. One by one, the older monks came to think as the abbot did ; the majority however, still insisted on Serafim working full time. He complied with their wishes but, with the abbot's permission, spent the night in his distant hut in the woods, praying and meditating.

Late in September of that year, he was ordained priest, and for more than twelve months officiated daily.

Then Pakhomius fell gravely ill, and Serafim begged to be allowed to wait on him and nurse him. It became one of his duties to receive the abbot's visitors and talk to them before they were admitted into the sick-room.

On a day when Pakhomius seemed a little better, they learnt from the rich landowner, whose son had thought them so odd, that the ageing Catherine, horrified and dismayed at the French Revolution, was abandoning her former ideal of enlightened absolutism; her friendship with Prussia grew closer; the country was not happy under her rule, private printing presses were closed down, the number of books published had declined; but Europe admired her and called her Great. In France, Robespierre had been killed. Paris, silent and gloomy for long, now freed from fear, went drunk with frivolity.

The abbot lay silent for many hours. Then he expressed the wish to see no more visitors. Turning to Serafim, "You nurse my body well," he said, "but it's my soul that seeks your comfort." "Father, my life is yours, do with it what you will." "Take Divei over from me. Take it over to-day." "Yes, Father."

A few days later, Pakhomius told the monks he thought Isaiah would make a wise, kind abbot for them; gave Serafim his blessing for the solitary life, adding, "Gird yourself for the fight, my son, gird yourself well"; then, he took the full habit.

Pakhomius died on a golden day in October. In the bright blue above, neat triangles of migrating birds headed south. In the quiet whitewashed cell, Serafim, Joseph, and Isaiah knelt by the bedside of their superior.

When the burial ceremonies were over, the monks, complying with Pakhomius's wish, unanimously elected Isaiah. Publicly, the new abbot confirmed Pakhomius's blessing of Serafim for the solitary way, but when they were alone the gentle, almost timorous new abbot said, "He gave you his blessing for the fight, but there's no need to go yet. The rigours and dangers are great. Stay with us. We want a librarian."

" I will go, Father. I'm not afraid." In the firm resolution of the younger man, Isaiah still detected a touch of the age-old pride sown by the devil, nursed by Adam. He sighed.

On December 2, 1794, exactly sixteen years after Serafim's arrival at Sarov, he asked leave of absence. With a loaf of bread in one hand, his Bible in the other, and Agatha's brass cross round his neck, he set out alone for his hut in the woods; a tall and stalwart figure, clothed in the simple black habit of the Russian monk.

THE FIGHT

EARLY winter dusk slowly clouded round Serafim. The blinding sheets of snow dimmed to gentle grey. The silence was no longer a mere lack of sound; it filtered through everything, communicated a new life to all; raised all on to a new level.

Towering, flesh-pink trunks crowded more closely together. The path that he had trodden down some time ago was hardly discernible. Spoor of wolf and wild cat crossed it here and there. He smiled joyously. Winter would guard his solitude.

Pakhomius had darkly insisted that the path of a monk living in a community is easy—a life spent in fighting pigeons, compared with the path of the solitary which is hard and full of danger as a lonely fight in the heart of the taiga.* The old man had not known, had obviously never experienced, the sweet force that complete silence pours into man: an exaltation which no human companionship can give.

Serafim stopped, avidly listening to the muted joy

* Siberian forest.

around him. No, in him. No. Yes. Where was it then? He laughed softly. There were no limits; there was no " in," no " out." He, the world, and it were one. Throwing back his head, he gazed lovingly into the distant pale green sky, spread out far away, beyond the white tops of the trees. Overflowing with sweetness, he sang creation's praise of its creator. Silly, simple little words streamed from his smiling lips. The servant was become the lover.

As the glad days slipped by, he wondered even more at Pakhomius's mistake. Solitude was not fearful. It was the very source of joy; there were the life stories of the Fathers, of course; but these men lived long ago, in a different land, in a heathen world barely waking to Christianity. They themselves were different too. He didn't feel about things as they had. There was a difference. And Pakhomius had made him lose sixteen years of bliss!

He followed the strict rule, day and night. Between times, he laboured physically, felling trees and cutting wood. While thus occupied, he kept his mind empty of thoughts, intent on the publican's prayer, which the Russians call the Jesus prayer.

Back in his hut, he pondered on the Bible, seeking to immerse his mind in the word of God, as completely as his heart was coming to be one with all creatures.

Every Saturday he walked to Sarov in time for evensong, slept there, had communion at early mass, and stayed for a few hours in an unoccupied cell where the abbot and others came to seek his counsel. His health improved; his wisdom, kindness, and insight increased. On Sunday afternoons, as the bells called the monks to vespers, he fetched his week's bread at the bakery and returned to the hut.

Spring came all too soon. The snow melted, the floods subsided, the hut was no longer inaccessible. He set himself to reclaim a patch of ground from the forest and made a kitchen garden of it, using moss from the thickets for manure. A little later he set up bee hives.

The woodland round the hut was hilly ; the banks of the Sarovka were abrupt ; the glades, full of flowers. He gave his favourite spots the biblical names that he thought suited them best, and went from one to another, to read or meditate. In Nazareth, he sang litanies to the Mother of God ; on Golgotha, he read the Little Hours ; in Bethlehem, lost in contemplation of the Holy Child, he sang the Gloria ; he went up Mount Thabor to meditate the Transfiguration, and up a high, steep hill overhanging the river Sarovka, to read the Sermon on the Mount.

As the summer advanced, two well trodden paths appeared winding between the trees ; the Sarov path and the path from the villages. Streams of peasants came to ask for guidance, and to share their sorrows with the hermit. They were careful to come when he was not at prayer in the hut, but working in his garden or apiary.

Grisha too, passing that way and hearing of a man of God great in wisdom, went to the hut " for a spot of soul saving conversation." He had aged, but his sight was still keen and, as he came out on to the clearing on the hill top, he recognized Prokhor in the hermit Serafim.

As always during work, the solitary was intent on inner prayer. Presently, his mind got the better of his body ; the hoe dropped to the ground. Arms raised, he stood rapt in contemplation. Grisha remained where he was, at some distance from the vegetable beds. Time passed. The hermit never moved. The sun slipped some distance down the sky. Muttering, " Queen of Heaven, protect the seeker from the evil tongue," Grisha turned and went his way.

The fool was not the only one to come upon Serafim rooted in his garden. Others saw him there, not noticing them, having lost contact with the material world.

One afternoon, two monks, who were hostile and

envious, went to the hut on an errand. As they drew near, orange and red splotches, bright against the dark green beyond, attracted their attention. Two village women stared at the motionless Serafim. Then the monks heard one woman whisper, " Look, I see a light round his head." The other whispered back, " It's his hair, I think. In the wind and sun, you know. Or . . . is it ? "

The monks exchanged glances of horrified disapproval. The women had not time to wait. As soon as they left, the monks hurried back. The monastery public opinion began to rumble. Coils of suspicion dragged, clanking, from loft to cellar ; self-righteousness stalked in at open doors ; surmise slithered through key holes.

Next Sunday, after mass, Isaiah led Serafim to his own cell. Shyly he said, " Scandal is spreading." He added with distress, " The confessors say the monastery is swept with waves of unclean thought ; your life is the cause of it ; your life is leading weaker men into the temptation of wrong thinking and wrong feeling." He concluded firmly, " You must stop women coming to your hut."

Serafim went back without his weekly ration of bread : he would henceforth limit himself to vegetables and honey. His heart was heavy, and he moved slowly. Even among the trees the heat was stifling. The drought, foretold some time ago, already paralysed the land with its fiery breath. And it was now, while this foretaste of hell scorched the country, that he was told to ban one half of the villagers from seeking consolation. How could he do it ? Why should he ? Did they not see that he had outgrown the cruder limits of self. How dare they exact that he should now build up artificial walls between himself and this or that creature ?

In the hut he flung himself on his knees, begging for guidance ; but it was long before the gnawing pain in his heart melted, and he was free to hold his mind fixed on prayer.

Having passed from prayer to sleep, he saw beyond his walls angels, inundated by a light that came not from sun or moon. Like the monks of Sarov, they were busy felling trees; but some of them carried the great trunks down to the village path and piled them right across it; then all flew away. An old peasant came along, looked up at the tangle of trunks and branches, scratched his head, sat down, thought for a while, sighed, and went home. A young man came along, looked around sorely perplexed, sat down, sang a snatch out of a melancholy chant, scratched his head and went home. A band of children came gaily skipping and running. Some held hands, others played hide and seek among the trees and bushes. For a minute they stared silently at the huge, bristling wall that had sprung up over-night, then drifted away to catch butterflies and gather flowers. Two women came along, one old the other young; they stopped, and burst out talking without listening to each other; they too, turned and went home. The trodden grass unbent, stretching its blades up to the light. From right and left, heavy branches sought each other and mingled. Presently the path from the villages, the path that had offended the weaker minds, no longer scarred the face of the earth.

Serafim obeyed. He rose and with the first glimmer of dawn, blocked the village road to all.

The heat grew more intense. The visiting monks spoke of fires in villages; the working monks, of forest fires. Rivers were drying up. In the open fields, the parched earth cracked, exposing the breeding places of earth spiders. Even in the usually sodden thickets, the weaker plants drooped and wilted.

On a stifling night, a little after midnight, when Serafim was kneeling deep in prayer, the crackling of burning wood and the stench of thick smoke made him rise; red flames licked the window glass. Blindly he rushed out.

The deep blue night was hot, still, and quiet. Not a streak of red anywhere. A cackling laugh sounded beside his shoulder. " What sort of an owl is that ? " he thought with a shudder, wiping cold sweat off his brow. When the same panic drove him out again two nights later, he remembered Pakhomius's words, " Gird yourself, gird yourself well."

He had built his hut on granite, and now brought a pick from the monastery, to make a cave under the floor. The entrance to it was masked by the brick stove; no one would have guessed it was there. He hacked away at the hard stone until the cavity was deep enough for him to stand in it, and long enough for him to lie down. Then he made another hole, for ventilation. In this stone chamber, having blocked the entrance so that it would take time to open it again, he resumed the rule of the nightly vigil.

The stench of smoke, roar of flames, and thud of falling timber still pursued him for a while. But he forced himself to pray unheeding, and overcame his sudden and unaccountable dread some time before the drought broke, and one thunder storm after another flooded the country.

As winter came round again, his mind soared to new heights and, while his hands worked, he frequently sang chants of praise without being aware that he was doing so. The weather hardened; but, forgetfully, he kept his summer habit of unbleached linen, worn against the skin and caught round the waist with a piece of string. On his feet he still had the summer clogs of plaited bast and thin leather leggings, more practical than stockings; on his hands, leather mitts; on his head, the conical black velvet cap worn by all Russian monks. Wherever he went, he had the Gospels with him, in a canvas bag slung on his back. The warmth that now glowed in his heart every time he said the Jesus prayer, protected his body from the sting of snow, frost, and wind.

The animosity of a group of monks increased. When the weather got more bitter and he still appeared at mass, early on Sunday morning, in his thin summer habit, they muttered their disapproval: he was intentionally behaving like a freak, they said, to build up for himself a saintly reputation.

After Christmas, the disapproval became so strong that the gentle Isaiah gathered his monks round him for a discussion. " Let us speak out aloud. We must not go about whispering and muttering against a brother who toils on the harder path. What have we against him ? "

" Freaks himself, freaks himself," the more bitter ones called out, " Discipline him, Father Abbot, make him dress and behave as all monks do."

" Well, you know," Isaiah said softly, " at first I had thought it might be so, but the bitter Epiphany frosts have come and gone, and he still goes about quite happily. Look at his face: waxen since his first illness here, it is now getting ruddy, like a child's ; a flame under his snow-white hair. His hands too, are always glowing warm. No, no, brothers ; it doesn't look to me as though he was freaking himself. We must not commit the mortal sin of condemning God's grace as devil's handiwork. And his summer habit costs us less. Let him wear it all the year round, if he likes ; no rule forbids it. Let us praise God, and uproot the envy and hatred which keep our hearts glum and cold."

The hostile monks grew more careful ; but their envy was no less bitter for that.

Serafim, however, had little thought to spare them. The solitary path was leading him toward the great temptation : the abyss of self-destruction. His immediate task, on the way to the abyss, was to overcome the dread of fear.

A new circle of horror drew round him, getting ready for attack.

In response, a hitherto unknown region of his heart stirred, exuding dark fumes of terror; and his mind, laying hold of the darkness, reshaped—in spite of his resistance—the old, gruesome bogles of mankind.

One stormy night, his attentiveness to prayer was shattered by grisly sounds borne to him on the long wail of the east wind. "Lone fight in the heart of the taiga," he remembered in a flash, striving to regain his grip on inner concentration.

Then they came. Roaring, screeching, clawing at the outer walls, rushing at the door, slithering down the chimney. The great hulk of a bear peered in at the small window; his bloodshot cruel little eyes gleamed red in the dim light of the sanctuary lamp; his black lips curled back disclosing long vicious teeth. Serafim, with his eyes riveted to the faces of the ikons, his hands firmly clasped together, toiled to keep his mind fixed on prayer. He would achieve the subjection of the will to reason.

The tradition describes his wrestle with the dread of fear as a siege of the lonely hut by wicked spirits who, during the dark hours, wander through the world for the ruin of souls. The seige lasted for months. "At times, the Horror tore open the roof and dropped at his feet putrescent corpses which jeered, rattling their bones. 'Rust and dust,' the corpses giggled, 'rust and dust.' At other times, the walls fell apart and he knelt, unprotected in a whirlpool of contending elements. Through the crash of magnetic storms and the blast of blinding blizzards he knelt, his eyes fixed on the calm faces beyond the steady sanctuary light." As a storm-tossed seaman grips the slipping rope with his bleeding hand, Serafim kept his mental grip on prayer.

But on Saturday afternoons, he went up to Sarov, as usual. On one of his visits there, Isaiah again ushered him into his own cell. "I've such encouraging news," he smiled benignly, his face crumpling into creases, "They write from Petersburg, 'Any objections to Serafim's being appointed Abbot of Alatyr, and being promoted to the dignity of Archimandrite?' and so, dear Father Abbot. . ."

Under his white hair, Serafim's eyes flashed dark and blue. It was the hand of God. He was being relieved of the nightly horror, although he had not asked for it. Relieved in a way that perfectly saved his face too. Why did the abbot give that cackle? What was it? Where? Behind him? Outside the window?

His eyes dimmed. Sorrowfully he said, "I cannot. I'm in the thick of the fight. I can't give up half way."

"But we fight everywhere," Isaiah protested.

"Not like this," Serafim set his jaw.

"Well," mused the disappointed Isaiah, "it'll have to be Abraham then, I suppose."

At the solitary hut the fierce fight continued unabated. "The evil shook the ground under Serafim's knees and gashed the earth only a few inches away from him. Suffocating fumes tore up and coiled round. Unheeding, he knelt and prayed. The evil caught him up, as with a hundred arms; raised him to a giddy height and threw him down again with great force. On his hands and knees, he crawled back to his place before the ikons, and prostrated himself till his forehead touched the ground." His reason was mastering his vacillating will. In his mind and heart his prayer flowed on unceasing.

The final test lasted seven weeks. Then the forest round the hut, the air above, and even the rock underneath, rang with the carillon of Easter bells. The fight was won and he unhurt.

On the morrow Serafim said to a large crow that came hopping towards him, " By the Grace of God, the evil can directly attack only human hearts and minds. To harm man's body, it must use forces of nature or some creature of flesh, tenuous though that flesh be. If, under direct attack, a man keeps his mind unbroken, his heart undismayed—his body will remain whole. There is, of course, the one vulnerable spot. But, by the grace of the cross, that is protected."

The bird cocked its round eye, looked wise, and hopped away, sideways.

In November of that year, Catherine of Russia died, and was succeeded by Paul, her son, whom she had always despised as a fool, but whom others now feared as a madman. The new monarch was well aware that his mother had thought to exclude him from the succession in favour of his eldest son, Alexander. Further aware of the widespread approval this scheme met with among her courtiers, he resolved to avenge himself on those who had injured and insulted him. He would destroy them and all the work of her hands. Her ministers and favourites were scattered; the charters she had granted to the towns and to the gentry were withdrawn. He gathered into his own hands complete control of all the work of government. In the spring of the next year, a Manifesto forbade forced labour by peasants on their owners' land on Sundays and fast days. On the remaining six days of the week, their work was to be fairly divided between their own and their masters' fields.

The gentry were dismayed: was the Tsar organizing world-wide famine? But the people prayed fervently for their new monarch: was not their long lost freedom glimmering ahead at last? Was not a loop in time being closed, completed? Were not Times of Happiness coming round again?

In the meantime, in Italy, Bonaparte had proclaimed: People of Italy, the French army comes to break your chains; our quarrel is with the tyrants that enslave you; meet us with confidence.

Paul detested the Revolution and its men. But he admired good generalship. Attentive to the " Corsican's " successes, he tightened the discipline of the Russian army and, to the despair of his generals, lavished his attention on it. The result was grotesque : a monstrous *corps de ballet*, moustachioed, be-whiskered, bearded, gigantic in stature—or diminutive and clean-shaven when snub-nosed—was harshly trained for a grim performance, entertaining only to Paul.

While the army was drilled into a ballet of frightfulness, the rest of the population were ludicrously enough, treated as soldiers. Even the Church, whom Paul respected, suffered : the practice of rewarding church dignitaries with medals and ribbons was instituted and enforced.

On this issue, opinion in the Church split, as usual. Deplored by men of God, the innovation was eagerly acclaimed by climbers. In vain did the Metropolitan of Moscow, tears streaming down his rugged old face, beg on his knees to be spared the affront. " I'm a monk, not a knight ! Why this outrage ? " he sobbed, while the insignia of the Order of St. Andrew was firmly pinned to his habit.

Once the initial indignity was committed, the prestige of dignity became more important from year to year ; the value of humility was forgotten in high places. Some official thought it time to enmesh, in this sticky-sweet web, the Solitary of Sarov, whose reputation of saintliness steadily grew.

A letter by courier reached Isaiah. The aged abbot read it carefully. He felt very ill, and since it was early in the week, he sent for Zakhar, professed under the name of Jerome. With many detailed explanations, an important message was entrusted to this old friend of Serafim's.

As Zakhar plodded through the dark wood to the hut, his face was drawn into a disparaging grimace. His usually twinkling grey eyes were clouded with envy ; he pulled angrily at his little brown beard and, ruminating his grievances, sucked a strand of his moustache. Oblivious of the real world around him, he walked in bitter gloom, in a parched grey landscape of his own projection.

Only when he reached the top of Serafim's hill and came out from under the trees, did he realize how young a world he had stepped into. Smiling, it lay before him, very still and drenched with sunlight. The tender green of white-stemmed birches trembled against a stolid dark background of spruce and fir. Here and there, the pink trunks of pines shot up, far above all other trees, and triumphantly spread their stencilled branches against a background of misty turquoise.

Singing softly, Serafim emerged out of a thicket. In his hands he carefully carried a small red cat that whined like a child in pain. Its mauled hind paw was bleeding; Serafim must have freed it from a trap. A great wolf trotted by his side, rubbing its head against his skirt. The group turned towards the hut. Zakhar advanced in spite of himself, mindful not to be seen but wishing not to lose sight of them. By the porch, a bear danced about, carefully rolling a large trunk into place, so that it might conveniently be used for a seat.

"That's right, Michael," Serafim called out, "just a little further, just a little more, whoa!" he fetched a bowl of water and a strip of white stuff from the hut, and, sitting down on the trunk, dressed the wounded animal's paw. The wolf lay at his feet. The bear amused himself hugging a stout tree a short distance away; he threw back his head and his sensitive nose twitched: was that the smell of honey?

A heavy bee bumbled past Zakhar's face. With a catch in his breath, he ran back down the hill, turned off the path, flung himself on the ground and buried his face in the fresh green grass.

Long ago, in Kursk, he had loved Prokhor Moshnin, as

all of them had. As much if not more. Then, on their arrival at Sarov, all had changed. Prokhor himself was no longer the sunny boy of Kursk. And Zakhar, sensing the hostility of a batch of novices, joined them, with a great feeling of relief. Later, he carried on the persistent, secret feud that some of the older monks waged against Serafim. This helped him to throw off the humiliating subjection. With bitter glee, he turned on the man he had too much admired; believed the worst of him; was glad to do so. Mocked at him. Misinterpreted his words and actions. To Isaiah's message he had listened with a feeling of envy that hardened to gloomy cold hate.

How was it that the confiding cat, the wolf, the bear, the banks of various green, the turquoise canopy above, had shattered the hatred which men had helped him to acquire and nourish through twenty years? Freed of it, he wept with joy. Time rolled back. He was as he had been—young, simple, loving. Eagerly he went back up the hill to give the abbot's message to the man of God.

The two old friends sat side by side on the tree trunk. Except for the wounded cat, that lay sunning itself in a tidy nest of wood shavings, they were alone. They talked long.

"And so," Zakhar concluded, "if you wish it, you'll be sent to found St. Saviour's at Krasnoslobodsk. When I heard of this, I thought it a great honour. Now, I don't know."

"Not an honour, a heavy cross," Serafim sighed, "but not mine; the cross of another." Compassionately he looked at Zakhar. "Not mine," Zakhar recoiled, "not mine. I had coveted it, I confess, but now I dread it. Not mine, not mine," he repeated in anguish.

"Yours, of course, since you both long for it and dread it."

After the excitement caused by this offer and its refusal had died down, Serafim begged Isaiah to make clear to all concerned that his path was not that of a hierarch or a founder. He was a humble man of God.

" What is the freak waiting for ? " the hostile monks sneered. " Will the Holy Synod have to offer him a bishopric before he shows his hand ? " In vain Zakhar tried to convey to them what kind of man Serafim was. " So that's the way the wind's blowing, is it ? " was all he got from men who had been ready enough to acclaim him when he forestalled their wishes and put their thoughts into words, more witty than they could find.

Beyond the great forest ring, the mad " Paulade " swung on regardless alike of man's reason and God's will. The Tsar had taken the knights of St. John of Malta under his protection, and become Grand Master of their Order, creating thereby a perplexing situation : the leader of the Orthodox Church (a church that deemed Catholics to be schismatics) was the head of a Catholic organization subject to the Pope (who considered the Orthodox to be schismatics).

Paul's admiration for General Bonaparte had, by this time, dimmed and he joined England, Austria, Turkey, and Naples against France. Soon, the Russian general Suvorov drove the French out of Italy, then abandoned by the Austrians, retired and marched over the Alps into Southern Germany. In a rage at Austria's betrayal, Paul broke with his allies and quickly concluded peace with their enemy, France.

Russian soldiers (between wars), their sons, brothers, and fathers (during wars), came to the solitary hut where the idyllic life gently flowed on. They brought their sorrow and perplexities, and went away comforted.

Paul's Manifesto was leading to disturbances all over the country. It had not been the first step towards abolition of serfdom, after all : only a puerile effort to enforce a superficial glaze of tidiness over the seething ocean of unrest and muddle. The peasants who had misunderstood it, and were acting on the force of their misinterpretation of it, sent deputations to voice their grievances against their owners. The deputations were, by order of the Tsar, publicly flogged, and the disturbances suppressed by military force. Many peasants were killed and wounded ; whole villages were burnt and levelled with the ground. Peasants, young and old, sought out the man of God, and went away comforted.

Then Paul's insistence on the freedom of the seas brought him into conflict with England, and a troop of Cossacks was sent, quick march, south-east, to India. The expedition was so obviously unrealizable that a rumour spread : the Tsar's object, men whispered, was to exterminate the Cossacks, against whom he had a dark grudge. Their old men and small boys came to weep in Serafim's hut.

The pain and perplexity of all whom Serafim comforted, was thickening round him and raising bitterness in his soul. Men came to him for light, received it, and went away at peace. But they left behind, cast on the source that had revived them, their dark and restless shadow.

The entire country groaned. While he, devoted to the Trinity and the Mother, sought closer communion with God, others smarted under the scourge of sanctioned injustice and moral degradation ! The bitterness in Serafim, gathered to a haunting feeling of impotence. What could he do for the motley stream of men that poured to his hut ? for the poor who were oppressed, and the rich whom circumstances altogether beyond their control forced into the position of oppressors. As Serafim's understanding of their plight deepened, the magnitude of their suffering diverted him from contemplation of the implacable glory.

His prayers weakened, his depression increased. Agonized, he peered into the gulf of pain, and weighed his limitations against its might. He could but dress the mauled paw of a wild cat; the wounds of a bleeding heart he could not treat. Men's tortured minds he could not cure; he could only pacify the distressed, and tell them to submit. Sick with pain and perplexity, he questioned the divine intention. Why was the good in men mocked by events beyond their grasp? Why were the weak and the helpless confronted with problems they could not solve? How could they avoid doing wrong in circumstances that rendered them blind? Yet retribution followed; and blind, weak, even good men, reeled under blows too great, too numerous, too baffling to be resisted.

Reaching the depths of human misery, Serafim despaired of God.

He sat on the ground, under a tree, and stared before him, blind to the world, unfeeling for all but his own wretchedness. A young hedgehog ran out from under a spindle bush; stopped by the motionless bast clog, smelt it; and ran towards the vegetable beds. The man had no eyes for it.

A dark, cold abyss, that he harboured within himself without knowing it, had unveiled. Over the brink, two variants of his own soul hovered. The one was to be his for eternity, the other he had to reject; for together they held his entire future: the future that would come, and the future of which he would one day say, *it might have been*. In his greatest hour, his hour of the free choosing, melancholy ruled Serafim; he did not want to exert his will!

One of the two souls was a body of glory; it enclosed the constant prayer of glorification, the prayer of praise. The other, grown from a spark of original pride, was a dark body of blasphemy; streaked with gelid lightning of despair, it spread tentacles to embrace, to imprison, Serafim; and he delighted in the cold despair of its presence, in the anguish of blasphemous thoughts, words, and deeds. Curse God and die! Curse the creator for the agony of the created? Refuse the lure of warmth and light? And exchange soothing quiet for the stark reality of cold, abysmal darkness!

Separation from his body of glory—already grown golden—meant self-destruction; it would lead to the great death that is an icy joy—a falling headlong through the void which cannot be measured, the space which eludes definition. Is not such separation the greatest act of self-denial? The dark abyss within him had called to the body of blasphemy. And the void, that is beyond man's power of bidding or rejecting, yawned everywhere.

The golden body of glory, tinkling faintly with the echo of Easter bells, drifted away toward the gently sparkling river: it was the soul that had secured him the friendship of the beasts. But his power over them being established, he could now deflect it to greater ends. The entire power of his despairing love would be used for the comfort of man—the sole creature of whom God demands more than his best and more than his utmost. Man, whom heaven tempts by the vision of a great companionship and abandons, destitute, broken, alone. Man, who is hung between light and darkness, crucified on the tree of life by his creator.

No gulf yawned in the ground before Serafim as it had when, without knowing it, he was acquiring the language of beast and bird. Now the hell within, the abyss, led him to the outer hell, the void. As he followed with avid eye the downward trail blazed by the fallen—the ever falling—angelic host, abyss and void united, sucking-in his mind, will, and senses. Overcome by the satanic indraft, he was sped to the source of negation where bide dead men, addicted to self-love. But Serafim came there through seeking God and loving men. And there he found the Man who, forsaken by men and by God, descended into hell, thence to blaze the upward trail, the path out of hell into heaven.

The simple song of the lark died down; and the elaborate melody of the nightingale; the owl's call moaned through the night.

Is there no way of avoiding the decision, no hope of going on as before? Must the price of the solitary way be paid at the hour of the greatest dejection, and abandonment by all?

On the quiet hill-top the fierce battle of the free choosing went on. When the crisp voice of the raspberry bird greeted the waking world, the only one for ever crucified—the giver of life, who is ever given the cross in exchange for his gift of life—smiled down upon his friend. The weary hermit, dragging himself to the river, bathed his drawn and haggard face, aged overnight.

After mass, Serafim sought Isaiah in his cell: "Send a dray for the bee hives when the right time comes. I can no longer attend to them or to the vegetables."

The abbot looked at him earnestly, roughly understood his state, and said,

"I will see that you get food daily."

"Please don't. I'll manage. Please, I beg of you, keep them all away. When this is over, I'll come. You'll be the first to know."

Half way between the hut and the monastery, he found a granite boulder with a flat top. Here he prayed all night. At dawn, when other men were likely to begin moving about, he went up to the hut, picking the herb *snitka* on the way. It was not known to be edible but he found that it made a good broth and, in the autumn, gathered and dried enough of it to last through the winter.

He brought into the hut another boulder, smaller than the one he prayed on at night, to kneel on through the day. The wolf roamed round, licked the man's face and hands, howled and loped away to join his pack. The bear danced about in vain, hoping to attract attention, then sullenly went off to find himself a wife and children.

The body of blasphemy had closed down on Serafim. But not before his resolution was formed. The Jesus prayer, incessantly repeated while he knelt on stone with raised hands, would transfuse his carnal body with spirit; it would make of his body a place of light; light would shine into the darkness and destroy it.

Slowly, very slowly, the enclosing darkness was overcome. Out of the place called Serafim, the light of spirit shone into the enclosing body of blasphemy, causing it to loosen its grip, waver, fall away, dissolve. It took a thousand days and a thousand nights to achieve it.

In the spring of 1794, the old bear came fawning and begging to be once more accepted for a pet. Another, younger wolf wished to be the solitary's companion. Serafim resumed his former life. Again he went to mass every Sunday, again visitors to the monastery were allowed to go to the hut.

One day, a tattered, bent and white-haired fool ambled up the steep path. Serafim ran to greet him, took him by both hands, led him to the tree trunk, into a patch of sunlight.

"I came in the year they killed Tsar Paul," mumbled the toothless Grisha. "That abbot of yours wouldn't let me get to you."

"Forgive me," Serafim said shyly, "I was very busy; striving for the inner composition of peace."

"H'm," grunted Grisha, "you've torn up, and burnt, the root of pride, I see. That's something. But what I've come for is this : What are you, budding saint or whatever you are, doing about the Old Believers ? I remember our talks on old Isidor's grave as though it was yesterday. I'll be going that way myself soon. But what are you doing about the Old Believers ? "

" Nothing. I can do nothing."

Grisha jerked his head away crossly and, fiddling with his hands, looked sideways into the distance.

Very gently, an expression of wonder lighting his face, Serafim said, " We of the human kind were not meant to live as we do. But we chose it freely, in Adam's hour of free choosing, and forfeited our blessed togetherness with Him and with all. Now that every one stands alone, total separation has woven superiority into the fabric of our life. We're not only different as the leaves on a tree are different, but one of us has a superior mind, the other superior dexterity, the third a superior body. Every one is in some way ' superior.' And, God's sons by right, we choose to be the step-children of the Prince of Pride. So, inevitably, in every community, we have superiors and inferiors. Superior is proud ; Inferior licks his boots, but sometimes, sick of licking, revolts and is butchered. Or else, Inferior licks Superior's boots so well that he lulls his master into an evil ecstasy and deftly jumps on to his back. Then it is he who rules. They may even change places, but the pattern remains ; the evil pattern."

" The dust of pomp, the rust of pride," muttered Grisha looking up sharply from under bushy brows.

" As life unfolds, sorrow deepens," Serafim went on, " because only love from above and devotion from below, simultaneously reaching out for each other, can overcome it. But love is mocked by impotent hatred, through disobedience ; and the devoted are kicked and trampled down by the pride of those in power.

" We all turn away from the face of love, and delight in

staring into the glassy eye of the tempter. Of course we know nothing of love; how can we? And we will obey no one; least of all him whose love rains down upon us night and day; him, who loves men such as they are; not as we love each other, for what we seem to be.

"Yes, Mother Church should love the dissenters. But they must obey her. Either of these alone can only lead to fresh misery, new misunderstandings. When will the two streams meet? Who can tell? But you and I must pray."

"I don't like it this new stuff of yours; but—I understand," Grisha said grudgingly.

They walked together to the edge of the clearing; stopped and looked at each other nakedly, without sadness and without a smile. "We shan't meet again this side," said Grisha, and gave the younger man his blessing.

The three years of vigil on stones had brought on Serafim's old ailment; his swollen feet were again festering.

To tone himself up, he resumed his lonely felling of trees and cutting of wood. But he now trained himself in the discipline of silence and was resolved, no matter what happened while he was at work, to utter no words but those of the Jesus prayer. When he could not avoid meeting a monk or peasant who came upon him suddenly, he bowed low to the ground, with perfect humility, but left their remarks and even their questions unanswered. They understood.

The leaves of the birches were turning gold, the maples stood splotched with scarlet, the sky above was a deep bright blue. Birch wood is best for a log fire; he went round carefully choosing his tree.

Rhythmically his great axe bit into the wood. The steady thud, with its clanging overtone, carried far on the light air. His mind's eye, lost in contemplation of the sun of love, blinded his carnal eyes; his mind's ear, keyed to the word of truth, deafened his carnal ears; his body, no longer the tool of his dark soul, was the place from which man's shining soul reaches out to spirit in a glowing stream of praise. Stretching from earth to heaven, such pillars of fire—grounded in matter—sing. Their fire does not scorch.

"Why, it's the man of God, I declare," a drunken voice bawled by his side. A huge flushed face with matted hair and beard stared at him.

"His fawning admirers from all over the world bring heavy bags of silver and gold; he keeps it all in a pot, under the floor," shouted another, a squat man, in a red blouse.

"Come on, little father, into the hut and deliver the goods," a third sibilant voice commanded, as a heavy freckled hand caught hold of his habit at the neck.

In spite of rigorous fasting and his three years of complete physical inactivity, Serafim, at forty-five, was still a tall, broad-shouldered, strong man. Besides, he had his axe with him, whereas the three men were only armed with poles.

The evil, foiled in its direct attacks, was using its surest weapon, man. Without interrupting his inner prayer, Serafim raised his axe; his unthinking arms raised it.

As in a dream, he saw himself, a priest at the altar, cup in hand. Dropping the axe, he folded his arms and, still silent, concentrated on prayer. The man with the flushed face caught up the axe and, rocking with laughter, brought down the heavy wooden handle in a lethal blow, on the hermit's head. They kicked the senseless body the whole way to the hut. Tore up the floor boards and searched everywhere. Not a copper.

On the damp grass, the bruised and broken body lay crumpled and bleeding. Above it, a flight of small screeching birds circled, almost flicking the body with their wings.

Somewhere near, a bear roared as though in mortal pain. Seized with panic the men bolted into the thicket, tearing their clothes and hands on brambles in their hurry to get away.

Early next morning, five monks found Serafim where his aggressors had left him; their three poles lay scattered nearby. These the monks used to make a stretcher.

With fractured skull, injured spine, broken ribs, and torn flesh, he lay dying in the whitewashed infirmary. For hours Isaiah watched over the unconscious body. " Queen of Heaven, Mother of our Lord, must the worst of us always torture the best? " With his lips twitching, he wiped his pale eyes that had seen much human sorrow.

Over the bruised face that lay like a dead weight on the coarse pillow, there hovered a smile of perfect peace.

II. RETURN MANWARD

Issues from the hand of God, the simple soul

THE SILENCE

FOR seven days, Serafim's mind refused to re-awaken into a world of subtle strife and crude reasoning. When, on the eighth, he slowly raised heavy eyelids, he was conscious only of pain. For twenty-four hours he lay motionless, aching in every bone and every fibre. The leeches and bone-setters, called in by Isaiah from the nearby town of Arzamas, filed out of the ward for a hurried consultation. Amazed that he should be alive, they suggested bleeding him. Isaiah, an uneducated man, deemed Serafim had lost enough blood without professional interference, and could not bring himself to give his consent. But they insisted, assuring him it was the only thing to do ; and all slowly crowded back into the sick-room. Serafim, in the meanwhile, had drifted into a condition not unlike sleep.

" Out of the depths of space, the Mother of our Lord, robed as the Queen of Heaven, advanced toward him. Again the apostles Peter and John were with her. Coming up to his bed, on the right, she glanced over his body at the group of worried men entering at the door. ' Why do you fuss, you who understand nothing ? ' she said severely. ' I've prayed to my Son for the right to nurse this man back to life. Leave him.'

" As she receded into fathomless silence, Serafim opened his eyes and answered Isaiah's hesitant suggestion with a firm refusal. Shrugging, but impressed by the quality of his voice, the physicians left him. Four hours his body lay inert, while in spirit he dwelt in the realm of the Queen of Heaven."

She had led him along the path of obedience, the path of the ever willing handmaiden of the Lord. Deeply penetrating the enigma of obedience, he had understood the manhood of her Son, the Servant. Now she revealed to him the Wisdom of God in man, and in all.

As soon as his consciousness returned, he got up and hobbled slowly round the room. Every restored bone and fibre glorified its creator. That evening, for the first time, he took food : bread and pickled cabbage.

Although he steadily regained his strength, he remained a cripple for life. Bent and hunchbacked, he moved about quickly on crooked legs, but could only do so propping himself up with a stick.

In the new year, a rich landowner of the neighbourhood asked to see him on urgent and important business. Vasili Tatishchev was middle-aged, robust, well fed and well meaning. As he walked excitedly up and down the narrow cell, his voice rose to a high pitch, then fell to a mysterious undertone.

" God's judgment ! They themselves say so. Gave themselves away bawling it in their terror. And no wonder : a thunderstorm in mid-winter, and lightning hitting their three homesteads. No other, mark you, only theirs ; and them not neighbours ! Clearly God's judgment. I'm keeping them locked up in the cellar of my house. The dogs are loose in the grounds, in case they broke out. What do you want done to them ? Have them whipped, sold into the army, or sent to Siberia ? "

In Serafim's emaciated face, the eyes shone tranquil, and far seeing ; then they twinkled. " Is not God's judgment sufficient ? And a human addition redundant ? "

" What do you mean ? "

" Do you know what I would wish, as a compensation

from you, their owner, the man responsible to the Tsar for their conduct, and to God for their souls?"

"What?"

"Help them generously to rebuild their homes."

"Impossible! What a frightful precedent! They would all be crippling each other to get money out of me."

"Not unless they're mad. And if they are, they should be treated as madmen."

"Impossible," Vasili cried again. "I've come to ask you what punishment to inflict, not what reward. If you can't decide, I will."

"If you do," Serafim replied gravely, "I will be forced to take to the road, and do penance for you. And I had hoped to die here, as I was ordered years ago!"

"The old man was frightfully difficult," Vasili complained to his wife, "I tried to reason with him but he's a stubborn old thing. I had to give in and promise, against my better judgment."

"The mind of a man like that isn't like yours or mine," his wife comforted him, "things will surely work out right in the end. Don't worry."

Fresh news of war, unrest, and unhappiness reached the monastery through the increasing number of its visitors. Toward spring, Serafim, harassed by the turmoil, persuaded Isaiah to let him go back to his hut. After twelve years of solitude, he found it difficult to fit in with the exigences of communal life.

Isaiah, although anxious to have him by his side, gave Serafim his blessing to resume the solitary path and, at last, after a long, comfortless winter, the birds and beasts received back their friend, the man whom they could understand.

The next year, Isaiah, advancing in age and failing in

health, relinquished his abbacy. The monks unanimously elected Serafim. But, after a night of prayer, he refused, stressing that he had not yet reached the goal of his solitary path. Reluctantly, they elected Nifont, a second best.

"What is it then, this goal of yours?" Isaiah asked.

"I don't know. I was stopped on my way there, wrenched back. Now, only sometimes, in the silence, I begin to hear the word that can explain it to me. But I've never listened long enough. I can't, living as I do. So I don't know."

In order that Isaiah should not be entirely deprived of Serafim's company, the novices and younger monks frequently drove the abbot in a hand cart to the hut.

Once, on St. Elijah's day, they chanced upon the hermit, toiling up his hill, a heavy sack on his crippled back and propping himself up with his axe. When the two old men sat down on the tree trunk by the hut, Serafim dropped the sack to the ground. Isaiah saw it was full of stones and sand. The old abbot wondered but said nothing.

That morning, Serafim's three aggressors had appeared on his clearing. They were led by the huge one with the red face, who sobbed like a child. When Serafim ran forward to greet them, they fell on their knees and touched the ground at his feet with their foreheads.

"Forgive us, man of God, forgive us and tell us what penance we must do. Lord have mercy upon us! Shall we leave our families, journey to the Holy Land, chasten our sinful flesh under the monk's habit?"

Serafim raised them from their knees. "Go back to your families and your work; strive to be loving to your wives, children, parents, to each other, to all. You'll find it hard enough. Try to be of good cheer and to sin no more. I'll do penance for you, I'll carry your load on my back. Go in peace."

As the men drew near their village, "When he said

that, his face shone like the sun," one of them broke the silence, huskily. "And his voice was as gay as the voice of a bird in spring," added another, in awe. The third said nothing; he still sobbed.

But it was not of this that the two old monks spoke. An eminent statesman had been visiting the monastery, and Isaiah's peace of mind was ruffled. The statesman described great battles: Austerlitz, Iena, Friedland, and Trafalgar. But the Tsar Alexander had signed peace with Napoleon at Tilsit. It was very bewildering.

"He asks for guidance, this great statesman. Not only for guidance in his inner life, but for guidance in his Court life; they're so closely bound together in a man like that. But how can I guide him in his motley life? I see nothing clearly there, no matter how long I ponder over it. It's like looking for hours into a muddy stream which won't clear; I see nothing."

"We must listen," Serafim said softly. "If we listen to the silence, we may hear what they should know. Then, we can tell them. Their own lives are too noisy." His face almost touched his knees, as it always did now, when he sat on his tree trunk. This made it difficult to be certain of his words.

Isaiah died in 1807. No sooner was he buried, than the sympathy and understanding he had so diligently fostered, dimmed. The monks' old hostility against Serafim flared up with new vigour, and enclosed him in barren solitude. There was no one to stand up for him now. Joseph too had died long ago.

"Verily, they of a man's household are his worst foes," thought Serafim, waiting patiently to be received by Nifont. He was certain now, that his time to face the hardships of a new discipline had come.

The paunchy pompous abbot scrutinized the crooked

crank before him. Nifont was not at all sure of Serafim's maturity for the great discipline of silence. His nose, long, thin, and curved up at the tip, seemed specially designed to sense the way the wind was blowing. His beady eyes were sullen. He pulled at his sandy beard. But, not being the man to stand up openly for his convictions, he gave his grudging consent which, under the circumstances, took the form of a blessing; gave it without tenderness or enthusiasm.

His misgivings were entirely unfounded: Serafim's silence was more than a refraining from the uttering of words. All that language stands for was henceforth eliminated from his life and his mind. His intercourse with the birds and beasts was wordless. As time went on, his prayer changed.

This coincided with an increasing difficulty to cover the four miles to Sarov. His feet were again very sore. Before the snows began to melt, he dragged himself to the monastery for the last time. After mass, he went up to the abbot and the round of the older monks, bowing low to each as though taking leave. Into the hand of the cellarer he pressed a piece of bread and a shred of pickled cabbage, a silent request.

When the hermit failed to appear next Sunday, they understood that he would not come to the monastery any more and that his food was to be brought to the hut. Later that day and on every Sunday in the future, one of the younger monks took to him a week's provision of bread and cabbage. This monk sometimes saw the recluse but was not seen by him, since Serafim always kept his eyes cast down.

He still felled trees and chopped wood, keeping nearer the hut than in the past, and carried a sack with sand and stones on his back wherever he went. If a monk or villager whom he could not avoid meeting came his way, he would fling himself down and lie prone, until the intruder had passed. If insistent visitors called at the hut, he hid in his granite cave; the three roughs had failed to find it, and no one suspected it was there.

Men have two ways of communicating with each other : they speak, and perceive the pattern of human thought, they look into each others' faces, and gain vision of human life ; neither can be acquired second hand.

In communicating through speech, words are our instrument; an instrument, potentially, of great precision. Entering deeper into the realm of silence, Serafim completely stemmed the flow of words within him. Not only the flow of spoken words ; even the flow of words that well up in the mind. He joined the host which supplicates, lauds, and blesses without words.

His mute exchange of friendliness with the beasts, raised their mutual understanding on to a new rung of perfection. His prayer ceased to be a logical sequence of words. The name of Jesus, the essence of the constant prayer, ceased to be a word; it became the direction of his soul in its flight Godward ; the tone of his soaring soul.

The tone was Jesus. And the direction was Jesus. Tone and direction blended. The velocity, received from the initial impetus, heightened. When it reached the limits of the notion of speed, he entered a realm more perfectly still than any other. In this realm, his mind was trained to hear the primordial word.

When the ebb set in, and human life was once more spread out before his mind's eye as a concrete network of ordinary facts, the fabric of particular human lives appeared before him with its particular design ; the pattern that every one of these lives should follow was obvious to him. Men's mistakes—intentional and unintentional, in the present, past, and future—stood out as clearly discernible blotches and tangles. They disfigured the particular pattern of divine purpose.

Waves of lassitude and ill-temper swept over Europe and Russia. The monks of Sarov were quarrelsome. Nifont, their abbot, was losing weight and growing more irritable.

No one had seen the recluse for two years. He evidently made light of Holy Communion. Real recluses were not obliged to take Communion. But there was no reason why Serafim should be allowed such laxity.

Nifont called the Chapter, and put the matter before them clearly, without mincing words. A decision was quickly reached: Serafim was to be given the choice of coming up for Communion on Sundays and feast-days, as had been his habit, or of leaving his hut altogether, and taking up his abode in his former cell at Sarov. Abbot and Chapter would then see to it that he indulged in no irregularities. This was not only their privilege, it was their duty.

Haltingly, the novice repeated the Chapter's decision to Serafim, who stood before him, as always, with downcast eyes. Then, having put the bread and cabbage on the board that served as tray, and, without hearing a word from the recluse, he went back.

Verily, they of a man's household are his most persistent foes. But, if a man retires into the realm of active silence and thence looks at man-made situations, he understands all; he sees everything in a different light. But it takes time.

Obedience is the way of the monk. When, on the following Sunday, the novice repeated the Chapter's decision, Serafim gave him his blessing and walked back to the monastery with him. They kept silent. On arrival, Serafim went straight to the infirmary, then to evensong.

Next day was the spring feast of St. Nicholas. After Communion, Serafim had an interview with Nifont who, ready for remonstrances and recriminations, was determined to be adamant.

"Father Abbot," Serafim said slowly, listening to the forgotten sound of his own voice, " I come to ask your blessing for total enclosure. And for your permission that the cup may, in future, be brought to me in my cell ; that I may communicate unseen."

Unprepared for this, and at a loss how to refuse without putting himself in the wrong, Nifont acquiesced and hurried away. He had other, more pressing matters in mind: Russia entered upon the crisis which led up to 1812. The monastery teemed with visitors : poor and humble men seeking consolation ; courtiers, statesmen, and soldiers seeking guidance.

Silent, with downcast eyes, Serafim passed their throngs on his way to his cell. He understood their plight, but felt no urge to speak. The circle of his interest was narrowing, Narrowing to a luminous pin point from which he could not deflect his mind's eye.

On May 22, 1810, Serafim was immured in a small narrow, stuffy cell ; enclosed in bricks, stucco, and mortar. The beasts of the dark forest of Temniki lost their friend ; a friend of fifteen years' standing.

THE OTHER FACE

THERE had been a time, long ago, when Serafim's interests were multiple and varied. His thirst for knowledge was then all embracing. More recently, in his flight Godward, he experienced the vastness of the immutable, all comprising world of spirit. Now that his sphere of interest was narrowed to a pin point, it was right that the shape of his life should follow this narrowing down.

For sixteen years, the immensity of dense, wild forest spread around him, as though to the confines of the world of matter. Far above the highest branches of the huge trees, the blue sky melted, retreated, as he looked closer into it. His constant intercourse with birds and beasts led him beyond the limits of human praise, into the realm of joy, into the delight which all creatures have in their creator.

This was lost now, and he was immured. Outside the walls, beyond the low, smoke-smeared ceiling, an active community hummed, narrowing down the silence in the cell as much as the hushed forest and vast sky had expanded the quiet of his hut.

Two small windows looked out on to the busy spring. The pictures, framed by them, made his non-participation in the joy of the world more concrete. After winter's sleep, the fresh green world was beginning to flower. The air was laden with early scents.

Brother Paul, an obedientiary who lived next to Serafim, waited on him. The two cells shared an anteroom. But Paul never saw his neighbour. When he brought the scanty daily meal from the kitchen, he loudly recited the traditional prayer, placed the bowl of oat-meal or pickled cabbage by the door, and quickly retired. Serafim, face covered with a cloth, cautiously unlocked his door and took in the bowl which he soon put back. Not infrequently, the door remained locked, the bowl untouched. He drank cold water, and that sparingly.

The observance of the rule, reciting of the liturgy and reading of the New Testament (Matthew on Mondays, Mark on Tuesdays, Luke on Wednesdays, John on Thursdays, the Acts and Epistles on Fridays and Saturdays) introduced steadiness and regularity into his life. On Sundays, an officiating priest brought the cup. Kneeling inside his door, slightly ajar, Serafim, face covered and head bent, stretched out his hands. They were all the priest could see, as he gave and took the cup. The routine never varied. But all the while, the Jesus prayer, become the gate to contemplation, brought into the monotonous enclosed life a new quality, a new richness.

The second way we have of communicating with each other is by looking into each others' faces. And our faces are there, such as we know them, only for us, of mankind. Since no man saw Serafim's face, it came to be obliterated, wiped out of the commonality of human experience. For a while, it hovered before his mind's eye as he had seen it in Agatha's looking glass, years ago, after the game of *burners*. "Not mine, not mine that. The grotesque grimace of the Old Adam in its variant Prokhor. God's handiwork disfigured by the first man's evil will."

Never sharing a word with men, hiding from them his face of sin, the recluse retreated as far from human kind as a man can. Silent, faceless he knelt by the Gates. They fell back. Became a bridge: the golden bridge that spans the abyss of evil, and points man's way to his creator. Nothing can destroy that bridge. Built of radiant light, it resists alike the onslaughts of matter, and of the spirit of deflected purpose.

With the word ringing in his mind's ear, and his heart resounding with the name of Jesus, Serafim gazed at the golden bridge. Thus he had once stared into the reflected blue of his own eyes. But he felt no giddiness now. In the weaving light, he focussed the source of all light, and beheld the face of the builder of the bridge, the New Adam. Supreme intoxication of soul led him to the muted joy of perfect peace.

A new quality was being steeled in him. Henceforth, he knew himself blind to reverses, slanders, injustice. He could live among men with a new fearlessness; if it was the will of God that he should again live among them.

One Thursday in August 1815, Jonah, Bishop of Tambov, tentatively expressed the desire to see the recluse whose fame was growing. Conversing, he and Nifont slowly advanced down the winding white passages: two tall figures dressed in black habits. At the door, Nifont intoned the customary prayer. The door remained locked. Raising his voice, the abbot explained who was there. No response. He sharply required the recluse to come out. Still nothing.

"We'll have the door taken off its hinges, at once, your Grace. Such insubordination, such insolence!" hotly blustered Nifont turning his thin enquiring nose on his Bishop. Jonah found it difficult to pacify one so eager to oblige, and to draw him away from the forbidden door.

Serafim had been standing before the lectern. *In my Father's house are many mansions.* Longing to enter, he knelt, and prayed for admittance. A streak of white advanced out of golden clarity. It called. He followed. They crossed green pastures and entered the golden city, the realm of wisdom.

" He discoursed with the Fathers, gazed at the exultant faces of the martyrs, joined in the song of the angelic host." Five times Paul brought the daily meal and took it away untouched. When on the sixth day the recluse returned to earth consciousness, he had acquired the capacity to switch over at will into the company of the blessed who dwell in the golden city.

Many years ago he had conquered all covetousness. The little food he took, kept body and soul together but could not thicken his flesh or prevent his mind from keeping awake in the regions where his lifted heart now dwelt.

The joy, experienced in the moments of ecstasy, was so potent that even its memory brought intoxication. But, whenever conscious of his human nature, he was careful to remember, in his prayers, his three aggressors. And, since he no longer roamed the forest, he wore, tied on to his back under his habit, a heavy iron cross five inches long.

" One day, standing by the golden bridge, the Queen of Heaven said, ' How long will you limit yourself to these three ? ' ' My knowledge of the plight of others is small,' he justified himself. She sighed, ' You who've looked into the face of my Son, have you not read the burden of his love ? Open your ears and listen. Listen to their endless, weaving tales of woe.' "

A week or two later, in September of the same year, on a Sunday, Alexander Bezobrazov, Governor of the province of Tambov, stood reverently all through mass. But the grace of alleviation he had hoped for did not come. His heart was heavy, his mind in a turmoil. His wife, an insignificant little woman, knelt beside him, punctuating her prayer with frequent obeisances. What a fidget she was.

On the way out of church, he remembered Vasili Tatishchev's story—heard years ago—of a crippled crank who lived there, at Sarov; a man of God.

" Could we see Serafim the Hermit," he turned to Nifont. The abbot raised his nose, " He's a recluse now. Sees no one. Not even me. Not even his Grace of Tambov."

" But he can't refuse a soul in need of solace ! " the Governor retorted hotly. " Please, Father, let someone take us there."

" If you insist, Excellency. But I warn you, it's waste of time."

Brother Paul led the way. At Serafim's door he intoned a prayer. The door opened wide. Serafim, standing on the threshold with uncovered face, bowed low to his visitors; went back into the cell; stood before the ikons. The

Bezobrazovs followed. Paul, strangled with emotion, closed the door.

So this was the man, side by side with whom he had lived for years; the man on whom he waited. He knew, by hearsay, that Serafim was an old man, crumpled and crippled. But he could have sworn he saw a giant, with a face of pure light that would blind you, if it were not for those fathomless eyes of a deep clear blue.

Bezobrazov's feeling of elation and satisfaction at getting his way, was clouding. His wife sat on the only seat, a rough hewn stump, which mostly served as table. Standing beside her, he spoke volubly, beautifully; but there was no response.

"The Tsar's a changed man," he exclaimed, at last, requesting by a look the habitual mute support of his wife. "He said to me 'The burning of Moscow has kindled in my heart a new ecstasy of faith!' and so it has. A changed man. And a lonely one! They no longer understand his aims. No one does. He hoped to reorganize Europe in accordance with the principles of the Christian faith. The Holy Alliance was to be the means of bringing this about. He got the signatories to declare their readiness to treat peoples as members of a single Christian nation. But the English mock: a piece of sublime mysticism and nonsense. And the Austrians dub it a high sounding nothing. They work for more practical ends, these gentlemen!"

Puckering his high forehead grown higher of late, he stopped again, hoping for some remark. Waited. Smoothed his bushy, greying side-whiskers with a shapely hand. Looked at his wife for more encouragement. Waited again. Serafim kept silent, eyes fixed on the ikons.

"And yet," the statesman went on, "a cousin of my wife's, young and very artistic, who spends his summers in Poland, tells us that some poor Jews there understand the

Tsar perfectly. They say it's here on earth, by such means as this, that God's kingdom must be brought about in the thick of life; just like that. Then, they say, goodness will manifest everywhere, in the empty spaces between men. That is the Messiah, according to them. Forgive me, for bringing this heresy into your cell, Father, but it worries me. You see, this is really what our Tsar is striving after, this congregation of all men, with God binding, cementing all. And the Jews understand it, the Jews! But not our fellow Christians! They mock!"

A large heavy man, he felt cramped in the small stuffy cell with its closed windows and sea of blazing candles before the ikons. Would nothing make the recluse speak?

Serafim took an ikon off the wall and handed it to Bezobrazov, keeping his own eyes riveted on the abstract Byzantine features. To break the awkwardness, which began to weigh on him, the Governor murmured, " Not the face of an English gentleman or an Austrian aristocrat, is it?" And as Serafim silently replaced the ikon, and resumed his station before it, Bezobrazov added with the irritation of one vaguely frustrated. " A poor Jew, really, when you come to think of it." Then drifting back to his preoccupations, " Because of all the iron, arms, woollen cloth, linen, and other things needed for the army and navy, the State long ago started factories, and supplied capital and labour for them. But the output is insufficient now. Customs duties have been lowered, and still there isn't enough of anything. And now, the question is asked: Would it not be more profitable to replace serfs by hired labour both in industry and on the land. But is it a matter of profit, Father? Is there no better reason why men should be free. Of course, the country's ruined, and so are we, but still . . ."

To this at least, I'll get an answer, he thought. But

Serafim silently knelt down and, become God-conscious to the exclusion of all else, fell into a deep abstraction.

Bezobrazov nervously rubbed his long flexible hands. "Forgive us for intruding on your solitude, Father," he said, suddenly shy as a schoolboy; called his wife with the raising of an eyebrow; crossed the room on tiptoe; and gently shut the door.

The garden was autumnal. The bitter breath of dahlias lingered under the copper, purple, wine-red, pale rose, and golden foliage. The deep blue sweep of sky was fringed with a row of clotted little clouds, white as sheep.

Alexander took a deep breath; a great gladness welled up in him. A very simple, childish gladness; very restful. He tucked his hand under his wife's arm as she tripped beside him, "The Christ was a Jew, of course. Do you know, I never realized it properly till now. That cousin of yours isn't a Judaiser, my dear, as I've teased you! Forgive me, yes? And we must pray for a real freeing of men. What do we know of freedom? What do we understand of anything. And what does ruin matter if only through all its harassing meanness our motives remain pure." They drove away smiling.

From that day Serafim's door was frequently unlocked. No one could ever be sure of it, but those whose need was greatest always found it open. He neither spoke to his visitors nor looked at them but, standing before the ikons, listened carefully to what they said. When he knelt down and ceased to be conscious of their presence, they went away.

Among those who sought him most often, was Xenia, Prioress of Divei—the convent founded in 1780 by Mother Alexandra, at whose death Pakhomius and Serafim were present. The foundress, after twenty years of austere and secret discipline during which she lived alone in a cell put up on the holding of the village priest, was advised by the elders of Sarov to put up three more cells and to encircle the new hermitage with a high paling. Here, with four other women, she lived to her last day. They kept the rule of Sarov, worked hard, and prayed fervently. But she did not live to see the hermitage accepted as a convent. This happened under her successor, Anastasia, in whose time the number of nuns and novices rose to fifty-two. When, however, at Anastasia's death, the nuns elected Xenia, Divei's troubles began. The new prioress was a fierce Christian, without pity for herself and hard on others. Her exactions incensed the sisters and they began to leave; presently only twelve remained.

The Sarov monks, who during Serafim's years of solitude and enclosure kept up the tradition of directing Divei, were unable to cope with the situation. And, as soon as the opportunity presented itself, Xenia dropped her long and fruitless talks with them for short soliloquies in Serafim's cell. Time passed. The nuns found her less rigorous; she was easier to please; the departures ceased. But now relations with the Chapter of Sarov grew very difficult; which made her in turn redouble her own austerities; and revert to greater severity with others.

"They don't really fear the devil, and they don't really understand that it's a privilege to tread the rigorous path," she complained to Serafim, dark eyes flashing in her finely chiselled face. "If I could, I'd put every one of them through every single step of our dear Lord's agony; then they'd begin to understand."

Erect and motionless this side of the golden bridge, Serafim heard every inflection of her passionate voice. But in his heart the voice of the Queen of Heaven resounded, "How can you listen in silence, have you no pity on my girls, do you know nothing of love? Curb her pride! My Son's life on earth was his alone. Not theirs, nor hers. My Son's servants do follow his path ; but they follow it in spirit, not in the flesh. Bethlehem, Nazareth, Jerusalem, Gethsemane, Calvary, all men can live them in their own souls. But no other feet can tread my Son's way. Put this into words that she can understand."

Turning, he came up to Xenia ; looked at her so directly that her eyes wavered and her eyelids dropped. " We must strive to make our bodies into friends of the spirit that longs to work through them. This is not achieved by copying the visible pattern of Christ's life ; only by the dedication of our own. The visible pattern of every single life is of God's choosing. We only have to become conscious of it, follow it courageously, and see that we don't distort God's intention. No two leaves on a tree are perfectly alike. Neither are any two lives. Every one must strive to fill this unique life of his own with a love of God so constant and so great that it flares up into a luminous love of man. Why do you not love my Lady's girls more ? How can I send the child Mary to you if you know so little of love and wish to teach St. Mary's girls the fear of the devil ? to teach them to be afraid where no fear is ? Listen, my joy, we elders and priors must learn to feel, discern, and understand. This only comes through long years of reflecting about good and evil. Then we see things, good and bad, in the light of His wisdom : and then we develop the gift of true discrimination, without which no man dare discipline others ; then we see through the wiles of the devil. Try to see how the pattern behind the events of to-day is transformed into the pattern behind the events of to-morrow. This is the way to defeat the devil's tricks. But then, how can we fear him ? No, no, my joy, he who loves God, loses all fear of the devil. You see, the devil is helpless against those who face him such as he really is. Terrifying he is, but only our own sloth prevents us from facing him without fear. As to fear of God—that fear is known only to those who can detect God's hand shaping the lives around them. Work hard, my joy, get ready to show the way to the child Mary."

Overpowered by this onrush, she automatically asked for his blessing and left the cell. It was not till late in the evening that she focussed the details of his stream of words. What did he mean by the child Mary?

The news of Serafim having at last broken the seal of silence—after thirteen years—spread like fire. Divei, Sarov, the neighbouring villages and the district town, heard of it within a week. Although he still kept to his cell, the routine of his life was changed. Every morning at eight, after mass, he unlocked his door and people streamed in: monks, nuns, priests, townsfolk, villagers, men, women, children, rich and poor. The door remained unlocked till eight at night.

It was on a still, grey day that Bezobrazov brought the tidings to Nooch, where Michael Mansurov lay ill of an incurable disease. He was a soldier and had long been stationed in the north west, in Livonia. There he married Anne Erntz, a Lutheran. Soon afterwards, a strange affliction visited him. His feet and legs swelled, and next their flesh and bones began to perish. Unfit for active service, he retired to an estate he had inherited thirty miles south-east of Sarov. His only comfort was in Anne's selfless devotion. Though attached to her family, she willingly left her native town. Pretty and jolly, she abandoned all amusements for the sick chamber. "A grand woman," thought Bezobrazov.

The dove grey air was saturated with fine soft rain. Foliage, tree-trunks, grass, roofs, walls, palings, glistened dripping wet. The hoofs of the three horses, harnessed side by side in a row, squelched rhythmically.

"I must get him to go to Sarov, I know I must,"

Bezobrazov thought. "Since no physician can help him, the man of God must teach him perfect acceptance, the joy of consciously submitting to God's will."

A few days later, two of Michael's most sturdy servants carried him into Serafim's anteroom. Aflame with tenderness and compassion, the crippled monk hurried forward to meet him. Michael slipped out of the supporting arms and threw himself on the ground, "Help me, Father, help me," he sobbed. Serafim, bending down, and gently touching the dark head that rested by his bast clogs, asked, "Do you believe in God?" "I do." "Do you believe in his omnipotence." "Yes, Father." "And do you believe in the boundless compassion of his love?" "I do, indeed."

"If such is your faith," said Serafim, raising the distraught man's face in his warm hands, "see the bond between him and his creatures. Believe that he can heal you, believe firmly. Poor Serafim will go and pray."

He hobbled back into the cell. At last he came out, in radiant stillness. He carried a small vessel with holy oil, taken out of the sanctuary lamp before the ikon of Our Lady of Tenderness: an ikon of the Mother without the Child, which had been with him through the days of his solitude; he called it the Joy of all Joys.

"Take off these wrappings," he said softly. And, gently rubbing the oil into the disfigured legs, added, "By the grace granted me, I heal you. You are the first I heal." Then, he brought a pair of hand knitted woollen stockings given him by a woman on the previous day and, adjusting them carefully, put them on Manturov's legs. He filled the sick man's pockets with little bits of rusks, and said, "Now walk over to the Guest House and hand these to brother Paul."

"But, Father, I haven't walked for years," Michael protested shyly, "I can't."

"Of course you can," Serafim laughed. "Come on."

Fearing pain, Michael haltingly rose from the floor and gingerly changed his weight from one foot to the other. There was no trace of pain or weakness. With a cry, he fell on his knees before Serafim.

"Get up at once," the cripple said frowning, "can Serafim take or give life, hurl man into the abyss of suffering or raise him to the peaks of joy? I do the will of my Lord. He, in his graciousness, is attentive to the prayer of his servant. Give praise to him and to his mother."

Soon after this, a woman, unhappy in her married life, sought consolation of him. Her thirteen year old sister, dressed for a long drive, joined her in the porch.

"What's this, Mary?" she asked.

"I'm coming too."

"Oh no. I've serious things to talk of with him."

"So have I. I must. And I promise not to listen," said the child hugging her.

"Oh well, come on then."

"Little vessel of God," Serafim greeted Mary as she crossed his threshold, "you're going straightaway to join Mother Alexandra's girls, aren't you?" And as she kissed the warm hand that fondled her head, he turned to the sister, "Take her to Divei, at once. Tell Xenia you've brought the child Mary from me. She'll understand. And *she*," patting the child on the cheek," she and I will both pray for you. Love, joy, happiness will return to your home. Go in peace."

Mother Xenia understood, but marvelled greatly.

Anne Manturov's joy at seeing her husband get out of the carriage, mount the porch steps and cross the whole length of the room with outstretched arms, overwhelmed her.

Tired, weeping, she stayed in bed for days. One morning, gazing out with feverish eyes at the monotonously drifting snow, she said, "You must go to him. We must ask how to thank God fittingly for his kindness. All your suffering, all my worry, wiped away in a trice," and again, burying her face in her pillows, she wept.

When, that afternoon, Michael entered the cell, Serafim left his other visitors and, crossing over to him, said, " The time has come to thank God by deed."

" I've come to ask how."

" Give him all you have. Take up the cross of poverty."

Michael listened aghast. How could he do this with Anne as delicate as she now was. " Don't worry about that," Serafim guessed his thought. " The Lord is merciful. You won't be rich but you'll never go hungry."

In a wave of enthusiasm, Michael promised. But, when the sledge turned into the familiar drive and he saw before him the old house that had long been in the family, his heart sank. Poor Anne—how would she take it—what had he done—there was no going back now—what had he done!

As he entered her room, she rose to meet him. " Well ? " she asked eagerly. Taking her in his arms, he told her gently, hesitantly; anxiously looked at her upturned face. She was laughing. Disengaging herself, she danced round the room, like a child, clapping her hands. Then, side by side on the sofa, they soberly discussed how best to set about selling everything.

From childhood, God was Serafim's constant joy; later, God became his one preoccupation. As he matured, preoccupation grew to love. Become too great for a human heart to contain, love now overflowed manward. His longing to let his new joy revive the arid, warped, grey lives that wilted round him, grew to the intensity of a parching thirst. But the slaking of it sapped his vitality.

For twelve hours, day in day out, they came to quench this thirst of his, and to drink of his love. A fair exchange it would seem ? But he was only a man. As the door closed on the last of them, he sank to his knees by the golden bridge and drank of the one draught that could restore him. And every day, after the communion of contemplation, his love and endurance were made greater than the demand.

As he gazed at the Face, his arms stretched out manward. Unrestrained abundance streamed from him to all. There was no self-will in him to dim it. Obedience, wise, long sustained, had burnt up the root of his evil will and its inevitable outcrop, pride. All the will that remained in him was a steadfast, clean resolution to do the will of his Master.

But his body was that of a very old cripple, and the regular din, turmoil, and stuffiness of the small cell, soon brought on his old headaches.

One morning, the novice John, out on his watchman's round somewhat earlier than usual, was perturbed to see an indistinct figure slowly creeping to and fro in front of a small side door that led into the passage by Serafim's cell. " An evil doer ? A thief ? What is he up to ? " Mustering his courage, John crept nearer. " The recluse ! " he gasped not believing his eyes. Reciting under his breath the customary Jesus prayer, Serafim hobbled about carrying logs of wood from one neat pile to another. " So ! Taking exercise, are we ; in the open. Sneaking out while others watch and pray," ironized John as he retreated into the thinning shadows.

That day the wave of visitors brought Helen, Michael Manturov's sister, into the stuffy cell. Attractive, gay, and wayward, this twenty-year-old girl had led a giddy life that horrified her elders but which her contemporaries strove to emulate.

Having become engaged, at the age of eighteen, to a charming young man with whom she seemed much in love, she broke off the engagement soon after the date of the wedding had been announced. Her relations' reasoning moved her no more than the passionate appeal of the deserted young man; overnight, she had come to see that far from charming he was altogether revolting, repulsive, impossible; there was nothing more to be said. But, to fill the gap in her life, she flung herself into a turmoil of excitements.

The gay round was interrupted by her grandfather's death. It fell to her to see to the funeral, make all arrangements, go through reams of closely scribbled note books tightly crammed in all his drawers.

The dismal task over, she and her maid got into the old barouche, her manservant climbed on to the box beside the coachman, and they trundled back to Nooch, her home since her parents' death though she was hardly ever seen there.

The lumbering vehicle jogged on to the rhythm of a lullaby. Arrived at a wayside inn, the girl sent off her servants to get a meal, insisting that they should take their time. She wasn't hungry.

Presently, alone in the snug closed carriage, she dozed. Through the veils that shrouded her consciousness, a great agony gripped her heart. Seized by sudden panic, she opened her eyes wide in a horrified stare, wrenched open the carriage door, and stared up fascinated.

The evening sky was a sea of colour. Between dark violet splotches of heavy cloud, daubs of orange glared fiercely. The molten fire rippled; a shudder passed through the clotted clouds. Parts of these darkened thickly. The darkness coiled, circled, swooped; tongues of flame preceded it, were blown forward by it, rushed at her upturned face.

Frozen with horror, she cowered, speechless. As the first clammy coils touched her, "Queen of Heaven," she called in her fluttering heart, "save me! I dedicate my life to you!"

Tripping back gaily after a hearty meal, the maid found her young mistress rigid, only half alive. Scared, she called the village priest. Helen, staring at him fixedly, slowly regained sufficient self-control to confess her misdeeds, and have Communion. But she refused to continue her journey that night, and kept the priest by her side till morning.

Back at Nooch, she explained to Michael—inexpressibly weary of her fads—that the whole of her, from the core of her heart to the edges of her mind, was quite different now. Her one desire was to become a nun, and she was seeing Serafim about it, at once. " So real, so implacably real," she kept interrupting herself and others, " So real, so implacably real ! "

When she entered the cell, Serafim wagged his finger at her in mock reproof. " How now, my beauty," he laughed, " what do you mean by keeping your bridegroom waiting all this time ? Your betrothed, with whom your will must one day be perfectly blended. Shame on you."

" I don't want to marry. I can't, now," she protested, taken aback.

" What a very naughty thing to say," he teased, " I've got the most lovely one of them all waiting for you. I'll tell him of all your virtues straightaway. Such a resolute girl, so wholehearted, unflinching, indomitable, ready to sacrifice all without turning a hair. Just the bride he longs for."

" I shan't, can't, don't want to," she sobbed.

" Come, come ! "

She returned home dejected and, with her brother's consent, retired to her room, there to lead a nun's life.

Michael and Anne were too full of their own future to mind or interfere. Their possessions were selling at a good price. Part of the money they gave to the poor. The rest Serafim wished put aside for future charities. Only a small portion was spent immediately on forty-five acres of land near Divei. Years later, this was handed over to the convent.

When the time drew near for them to leave the house, Michael unexpectedly got an offer from General Kuprianov to become his agent. " He's most generous about it," Michael explained to Serafim. " But it's tumbled on to me so suddenly, out of the blue, and it would take me further from you. Besides, I've never done that kind of work. I'm a soldier."

" But just think, you'll change your sword for a ploughshare, Mika ! " Serafim exulted. " Of course you must go." And he added slowly, as if listening to something he alone could hear, " The peasants are so unhappy there. Terribly unhappy. So unhappy that their lives have come to reek with sin. They'll learn to love you. They'll obey you. You'll be the means of their return to better ways. Don't waver. Go. Make haste."

" And what shall I do with my sister ? "

" Send her to your aunt for a while. She can practise her self-imposed rule there. It's not for long anyway. Not for long."

Serafim's joy—the joy of the creature that constantly gazes at its creator—was so full that he sometimes thought it must tear down the walls of his cell. They stood stolidly. And so he left them from time to time in the dead of night, and ventured beyond the Sarov walls to roam among hushed trees, under twinkling stars. But most of his nights he still spent in prayer, and his days were devoted to any one who chose to come.

All through these years of his return manward, the Queen of Heaven watched over him. Satisfied at last, that the enclosed life no longer was the true outer expression of the sea of love he was become, she visited him in his sleep and said,

"You can now openly do my Son's will. Come out of enclosure. Roam the forest, visit the hut; renew your friendship with beast and bird, your interchange of wisdom with nature. True will can now express itself through your words and actions, true love can shine unhampered out of the dwelling you have become."

Next morning, on December 3, 1825, Serafim, immediately after his early morning prayers, left his cell and sought Nifont.

The abbot was busy over his correspondence. When Serafim entered, he rose, unaware of what he was doing, and blinked his little eyes, usually shallow and sly. But as he looked at the joyous crank before him, his eyes grew kinder, deeper, more earnest.

"Mind your health, dear Father Abbot," Serafim said tenderly, "these liver troubles can turn very nasty."

Then, as Nifont mumbled indistinctly, "The Queen of Heaven bids poor Serafim wander about freely. Will you raise the discipline of enclosure, Father, and give me your blessing for the free life?"

Bending down, Nifont spontaneously kissed the radiant cripple, forgetting, for the moment, his old hostility.

Fluffy, gentle, slow, the great snow flakes tumbled, danced, chased each other round about him. The hoary, flesh pink pines stretched up on all sides, proclaiming earth's joy in heaven. They, her myriad arms, stretched heavenward in a movement of silent delight.

On the pure white carpet, the cripple's footprints mingled with the spoor of wild beasts. Twenty-eight years ago, on a day much like this, his Bible and a loaf in his hands, and Agatha's cross glinting brassily on his black habit, he had passed there, a resolute, stalwart, manly figure striding through the white hush to the solitary hut.

To-day, on the shabby, much darned white cassock that

covered the small bent figure, still glinted Agatha's parting gift. And under the cassock was another cross, of heavy iron, strapped to the crippled back. The crooked old man leant heavily on a short stout stick.

" Archangel Gabriel, winging his way round the outposts of infinity, chanced at that moment to look into space. Through a mist of whirling snowflakes, in a snow-shrouded land, among tall columns of hoary trees, he perceived a straight pink flame advancing lightly, resolutely, joyously, from the white walls of Sarov towards a spot out of which the light of a mighty human endeavour streamed heavenward. The light was timeless. With a flap of his wings, Gabriel retreated from the confines of space, and reported to the Queen of Heaven.

" She appeared to Serafim some two miles away from Sarov. Rising out of earth that was boggy in summer, descending out of skies that were still blue beyond the clouds, she wrapped herself in the soft greens and deep browns that lay hidden away in trunk and branch, under the crust of glazed hoarfrost.

" With her staff, she struck deep into the frozen earth. A pillar of sparkling water shot high up into the dove grey sky. ' The waters in the pool by the Sheep Gate made whole only one sufferer, once in a while,' the Queen of Heaven said, ' but my Lord wishes these to heal all who, loving him and revering me, drink of them or bathe in them their bodies, at any time and in any place.' Then, coming nearer, she communicated to Serafim, without further use of words, all she wished done at Divei. A little to the east, on a rise in the ground, Peter the Apostle and John the Divine stood motionless, listening."

She brought with her the breath of eternity, and Serafim, contemplating with new penetration the Wisdom of God in nature, lost all sense of time. Earth consciousness returned when, with dusk gathering round him, he found himself,

drunk with joy, dancing among the hushed, attentive trees.
With earth consciousness, the concrete love of men returned; and the weight of their sorrows. They would be waiting in his cell, as lost sheep. Desolate. Desperate.
Singing a new song of praise, he hobbled back to the monastery as fast as his crooked legs would carry him.

THE SIMPLE SOUL

AT sixty-seven Serafim had, at last, attained to a perfect blending of spirit and body, to a simultaneous life on two levels. St. Mary's obedientiary became the servant of the Queen of Heaven, he was entering on a new discipline: that of incorporating in his life, without destroying its harmony, the moving mosaic—the kaleidoscope—of thousands of other lives.

"When he raised his eyes to the ikon of our Lady, I bent my head, unable to endure the brightness of his face," whispered a woman who had come for consolation, and now lingered with other visitors in the monastery gardens. "He put his warm hands on my bowed head and went on with his silent prayer. A tear dropped on my parting. Was it for me he wept? A new sweet courage sprang up in my heart. My hard life will grow even harder, I know; bound to. But I'm not afraid. I can stand up to it. I can stand up to anything."

For a few days, he was left alone more than of late. People had not yet realized the significance of his having come out of enclosure. While he was busy re-enforcing with pebbles the banks of St. Mary's Well, they still crowded in his anteroom.

The weather was mild, and the Well had not frozen.

Passing that way with the child Mary and another nun, Evpraxia, he showed them what he had done and what there still remained to do. " How neat," exclaimed Evpraxia, coughing as she always did in winter.

" How carefully you've placed the pebbles; wedged them in so beautifully; their colours make a pattern too," Mary marvelled, bending down.

Serafim said, " Even we do things for men sometimes and not directly for our Master; then, our effort to do the bit of work perfectly is its dedication to him." Turning to Evpraxia he added, " Stop that barking noise, my joy."

" I can't," she laughed.

Taking off his leather mitt, and filling it at the spring, he bade her drink. The ice-cold water burnt her throat like fire. She gasped for breath.

As they continued on their way to the hut, he marked with his axe first one tree, then another. " These will go to build your mill," he explained. " My Lady wishes a new foundation to grow up in the heart of the old. And it's to grow up round a mill, a wind mill! ' My miller girls ' my Lady calls you. But don't speak of it yet."

" You'll let us help with the felling, won't you ? " they begged.

" Good," and he chose a third tree.

On the way back, they came across a young peasant, standing by the Well, and weeping. Every time he glanced at the bridle he held, he wept more bitterly and wrung his hands.

In these days, the Russian peasant's horse was his most cherished possession; horse thieving was a heinous crime, and the number of such thefts rose whenever a wave of increased nervousness and unrest swept the country.

Serafim hobbled up to the peasant, patted him on the shoulder, and said, "; Hurry to the fair at Lemet, there you'll find them. What a fine pair ! You just look straight at the man who's selling them, bridle them, and take them away." The peasant bowed low, and ran off, in a hurry to beg for a lift that way.

A few days later, another peasant, dishevelled and distraught, stood outside the cell relating his misfortune. "There he comes, down that path," someone pointed. The man rushed forward and flung himself at Serafim's feet. "Now, now, what is it?" the cripple asked, pulling him up. "My horse, my only horse, how shall I feed my family, how? You've the sight? Have you? Please, please find him, my poor dear horse. My poor, poor family."

They were standing at some distance from the others. But Serafim, taking with both hands the man's head, bent it down till it touched his own, then very softly said, "Make around you a fortress of silence. Go to the village Toos. As you come near it, turn to the right and pass at the back of four houses. You'll come to a little gate. Go in. There, before you, you'll see your horse tied up. Untie it, and take it home. And keep silent about the whole thing for three years. Keep silent."

The revolt of the Greeks against Turkey had inspired the Russians with great enthusiasm, since both nations belonged to the Greek Orthodox faith, and at that time religion took precedence over other matters. In the remotest Russian villages, the Greek cause was regarded as sacred, and prayed for.

But of late—and particularly after the Russian Army's return from abroad—a section of the educated classes were more and more attracted by the West. Young officers, interested in social and political questions, had even formed a whole network of study groups.

As the Tsar's disillusionment in his allies, and his doubt in the desirability of reforms, produced a leaden despondency, a bitter wind of discontent fanned the intellectual pursuits of the study groups into an activity of secret subversive societies. Alexander knew, but his tortured mind abhorred dwelling on it. His heavy heart bade him keep inactive, inert, and let things take their course. The general feeling of suspense, become unbearable, broke in the beginning of January, when news of the Tsar's mysterious death at remote Taganrog shook his subjects.

Had he been ill? No. Was he really dead? Who knows. But his coffin was empty, they say? No, not empty but the body in it was not his; it was the body of a soldier who resembled him, and opportunely died. Where was he then? Gone off, a wanderer, in search of the holy life; gone off to pray in solitude; gone off to expiate the Sin: mankind's, his country's, his own—implicated as he was in his father's murder. Implicated, he? Yes, surely you remember the names of the courtiers who strangled Tsar Paul, his eldest son's closest friends. Friends, yes. Yes, perhaps. Who's to be Tsar now? The next brother, Constantine. No, no. Constantine long ago relinquished his rights in favour of the third brother, Nicholas. You don't say so, I never heard of it. Well, they kept it dark. Why? Who knows. But Nicholas abhors the very idea of ruling, doesn't he? He does indeed, but Constantine has refused to rule; an official abdication, you know; regular, though secret.

Everything was going underground, and the numerous secret societies had amalgamated into two large ones: the Southern Society, all out for a Republic, and the Northern Society, which wanted a Constitutional Monarchy. But for practical purposes they pulled together.

While couriers rushed to and fro between St. Petersburg (where Nicholas was in command of the Army) and Warsaw (where Constantine was Viceroy) the Northern Society, playing off the cause of one brother against that of the other, raised an armed revolt in the capital. This was quickly crushed; in view of his brother's stubbornness, in accordance with the wishes of his ministers, and in compliance with his mother's entreaties, Nicholas let himself be proclaimed Tsar.

Life apparently grew more tranquil. Order was quickly restored, and next fixed in a rigid style not without austere beauty, and perfectly in keeping with the new Tsar's classical and precise mind. Against the rectilinear, unemotional background of this new style, the old native genius richly splashed deluges of colour, produced its usual cavalcade of originals and freaks, sang its nostalgic melodies. But under the framework of classical symmetry, and beyond the joy of pageantry and colour, disorder throbbed darkly.

The dark heart-beat affected all. Because of it, superficial characters multiplied their efforts to keep even more to the surface of things, while deeper natures entered further into the core and mysteries of human life.

The disorder was reflected even in the inner life of Helen Manturov, secluded in her aunt's house. Most families of the nobility had some member implicated in the revolt. Good people, all of them; some, outstandingly good. But their actions—misguided, rash, childish—had only led to evil, and the multitude condemned them.

As Helen listened to her aunt's lament, her mind was torn between sympathy for the men, and condemnation of their action. " I must advance further Godward, then I'll understand and find peace," she thought, " mere seclusion from my fellow-men can get me nowhere."

A few hours later, she found Serafim by St. Mary's Well. The spring floods over, he was busy digging. " Look," he called out as she approached, " here I'll plant potatoes, and there onions. A grand kitchen garden, isn't it?" Then beaming at her sadly smiling face, " You had thought of it as a running away, my joy. Now, you see it's a flight forward. Go to Divei; give it a try. We withdraw from men only to build the fortress which withstands their evil."

As her carriage slowly bumped and squelched along the road to Divei, trails of fleeting rainbow hovered over the dripping twigs, boughs, and branches thickly covered with pink, mauve, green leaf-buds, already sticky and beginning to swell. "Just another slight re-adjustment of my wishes, thoughts, and feelings, and I'll hear the whole of nature sing His praise." She was completely happy, perfectly at peace.

A month later Serafim sent to Divei for her. Again she found him on the same spot but this time a great crowd pressed round him. Catching sight of her, he took leave of all, making the sign of the cross over them, and led her to the Well round which a square wall of logs, two feet high, had been raised. Here they sat in silence, while the crowd trickled away on all sides into a bright world of flowers and song.

"It's time you were wedded, now," he said, "tell Xenia to give you the black habit." Then, as in a dream, "My Lady wishes the mill to be worked by girls only, by wise virgins. She wishes them to live there apart from all the rest: the widows, and the foolish virgins who are neither fish nor flesh, mere passengers. You see, my joy, in the silence we hear the word; faceless, we see the face; and the wise virgins fathom the depths of love. Lady Abbess," he said turning to Helen with animation, "take great and tender care of the child Mary; she's growing up so wise, so very wise."

"Abbess, me?" she gasped, "I can't!"

"Lady Abbess," he went on. "I would have you know that Mary is a jewel of which the miller girls will never find the equal when she's gone. You, and her, and Evpraxia, my Lady has chosen. She'll choose another nine presently. Twelve miller girls in all, she says. And she herself is, of course, your real abbess."

"But I can't be abbess, I really can't," Helen insisted, "any other charge of yours I'll gladly do, but not this; I can't."

"Other charges will come."

"I'll do them gladly but not this."

"This one we'll keep secret, my joy. It will never come out into the open. But in the secret pattern of things you simply are their first abbess on earth; the first abbess of my wise virgins."

"No, no. Not even secretly. Anything else. But not this," she repeated greatly perturbed.

All the summer of 1826, men and women thronged to the wild woods seeking consolation and guidance, begging Serafim for his prayers.

But as the white nights dropped their enervating, mistless pale green veils over tidy St. Petersburg, Nicholas of Russia came to a strange decision: he himself would cross-examine the ringleaders of the revolt, he would penetrate the workings of these enigmatic minds, gain insight into them.

The ringleaders, each in turn and time and again, were brought from the casemates and bastions of the Fortress of Peter and Paul, across the Neva, to the Winter Palace. The Tsar received them in his study. Of gigantic stature, and of exceptionally well proportioned and clear cut features, he was courteous, gentle, kind. Would he be generous? His one desire was to understand. The mood of tenderness in the imperial study often rose to such a pitch that examiner and examined almost wept in each other's arms.

In July, the five ringleaders were hanged. A little later about eighty were exiled for life to Siberia, to work in the mines. It was suggested that the wives of the convicted should be permitted to seek annulment. Instead, they petitioned to be allowed to follow their husbands. The

Tsar consented reluctantly. Out there it was no life, no climate for women.

The number of visitors to Sarov increased with every month. "We can hardly ever close the gates before midnight now," the watchmen groused. "But why must we shut them at all?" the hunchback asked, "How can we gain insight into the aching hearts and tortured minds of these seekers unless we open our hearts and minds, and gates, and let them unburden their sorrows to us. Isn't our work, our very life, wasted unless they can?"

John, passing that way, smiled disparagingly, "Sound philosophy for a monk! And why is the cup still brought to the freak's cell on Sundays and feast-days? What is Abbot Nifont thinking of?"

Next morning, a carefully worded letter went to the authorities concerned. The answer came to Nifont in the form of an injunction: since the *starets* Serafim no longer lived enclosed, he was to communicate in church, as every one else.

He went there fully vested, and, having stood motionless through the long service, came out blind to his surroundings. But, sometimes, descending the steep church steps, he would pause and address the crowd:

"God is the fire that kindles the human heart. The devil's breath is ice-cold. But only the waters of Shiloam, the waters that flow softly, respond to God's fiery breath. When, through hate and envy, the heart is drained of these waters man is but frozen dust. To behold the glowing face overcomes the enemy's deadly breath."

His voice had a ring of authority, he seemed to grow in stature, his piercing eyes flashed, and gazed into the hearts of the people. He walked back to his cell between hushed rows of reverent men, women, and children.

Next summer a very small hut was put up for him by the

Well. On week days he went there at about four in the morning and stayed till dark. He worked as much as his deformity and age allowed. In between the practices prescribed by his rule, for which he retired into the near hut, he dug, hewed, reaped with a sickle. As he worked, he spoke to all who came. Children swarmed around, helping ; or thinking they did.

Occasionally, he would go to the old hut for a day of solitary meditation ; and for deeper penetration into the mystery of wisdom in nature. On the way back, visitors thronged round him.

He hardly slept, lying in his cell on sacks filled with stones, or sitting on the floor, his back rested against the wall. Most of the night he prayed. As the lives of others became part of his own, his prayers of intercession acquired a new concreteness.

Paul, still his neighbour, felt it right to approach him with careful remonstrance. "Father, this sea of lights always burning before the ikons in your cell, and you so seldom there ! It might so easily cause a fire."

"No, no. It won't. Not for another few years. Then, fire will announce to you my birth, my death as some would say."

"But all these candles. . . ."

"I must have them. It's difficult sometimes," he explained, "I get so deeply concerned with the issues of the lives immediately before me that, in my weakness, I can't keep in mind all the others too. So there they burn, these candles. When one of them goes out, I know for whom of the absent I must pray. There are so many of them, and I can think of no better way. Their lives, the lives of these neighbours of ours, they are our very flesh."

He was gaining clear insight into the physical and spiritual fabric of the lives of others ; he understood their happiness or sorrow better than they did themselves. The tidings of his insight and foresight spread further afield.

Anton Kasatkin heard about Serafim from General Kuprianov, during the siege of Adrianople. On sick leave, and thoroughly disgusted with life in the army, he went to Sarov. His superior officers were all either mad or foolish, either hard-hearted or muddle-headed. He could no longer bear subordination to them. It only made him as bad as they were; reduced him to their level; and he was different; quite different; he would give up everything and become a monk.

His cherubic features pinched, his usually fresh complexion ashen grey, he appeared in Serafim's cell. It was a cold winter's day with nothing to do at the near hut.

"How do you know," Serafim asked, seating the officer on one of the window sills, "that you won't find your abbot just as evil as your colonel? Worse probably; you'll have more time to think No, stay where you are. And humbly work for the inner peace."

"But I've never been happy in the world, never!"

"You can't be, until you meet the girl you should marry."

"But I don't want to marry."

"Then you don't want to be happy. Listen, go to the guest house, there you'll find a mother and daughter. The daughter is your bride in the eyes of God, that's why the devil is working hard to keep you apart. Tell them I want to see them now, and bring them here."

Bewildered, Anton went to the guest house. Made enquiries. There was no one there whom the description fitted. Thoughtfully he wandered out of the gates. The snow crunched underfoot, the frost nipped his face. A large sledge came driving past, its silver bells jangling. In it were two women, carefully wrapped in furs. All he could see of them was the oval of their faces. One old and proud, the other young and very sad. "Them," he knew at once.

"Madam," he addressed the old one, his voice ringing loud and clear in the frosty, snow-shrouded stillness, "Father Serafim bids you and your daughter drive straight to his cell, without delay."

"Good gracious," she exclaimed with haughty amusement, "miracles already! Timothy," to the coachman, "do as the young gentleman says. We are expected." And to her daughter, "You're apparently going to have it all your own way. Messengers sent out beyond the gates to meet the cherished novice."

"Divei, Divei," breathed Sonia, closing her eyes. A faint smile hovered over her face, silent and far-seeing. But in the cell she wept bitterly, "I don't want to marry like others."

"You won't," Serafim assured her. "This marriage is of God's choosing."

"But I want the virgin marriage, like Helen," she sobbed.

"No, no. My Lord and my Lady have chosen the cross of the other for you. They want you to found a home where love blossoms into children, and into kindness and charity that spread far and wide. A Christian hearth is a rare jewel and an indomitable weapon. This jewel is yours to guard, this weapon yours to wield. Come, Anton, wipe her tears. Kiss each other." He joined their hands and gave them his blessing.

"But listen," intervened the mother, "I don't know this young man. Our family . . ."

"God knows all that's worth knowing about your families," Serafim interrupted. And, as she flushed, "These two can only be happy together, Madam. Whatever else they do, ill luck and a gnawing misery will haunt them.

Together, they'll bring joy to a host of others. And we do all need that so badly."

His years slipped by, increasingly filled with the worries and sorrows of other men. A complicated surface pattern spread over his inner peace. Like a dark and fanciful net flung over a bright globe, this pattern underlined, through contrast, the value of his own luminous life; enhanced its beauty through introducing a rainbow of colours; made it more vivid and moving. Most sorrows he shared deeply. But some he could not understand.

At the age of nineteen, the child Mary died, a nun of the strict rule. " Why do the sisters weep ? " he asked Helen as, once again, they sat on the edge of Mary's Well. " She died because, through God's grace and her own effort, she matured so quickly that she can already take her place in my Lady's train of intercessors. Constantly she prays for us. And how we need them, her prayers. The Wrath is nearing. Terribly will it visit us. Us, whom no outer foe can conquer. But the blight of the Fall, the blight we harbour in our minds and hearts may do so when the Fallen One spreads before us the temptation to be a temptation, the temptation to be a seeming good, loudly acclaimed, universally proclaimed, as good. Through the years of temptation, the wise child Mary will kneel, praying that we may be helped to choose the real good at our time of free choosing; praying that we may choose to be a blessing in the eyes of God, even at the price of being condemned by men; derided; possibly tortured; crucified ! "

After a while he added, frowning, " The blessing of such great and subtle temptations is in the door they open on to the realm where the seeming good and the real good may blend." And turning to her, " They can ! If men are ready to pay the price: loneliness, each one in his own

Gethsemane; stark abandonment by all, each one on his own Calvary."

John, passing by on his way from the forest to the monastery, stared superciliously at the couple. Helen knew how much he disapproved of Serafim's preoccupation with the lives of women, and, suddenly grown self-conscious, turned away and looked down into the well. "Father," she gasped, grabbing Serafim by the arm, "What is it?"

The spring, usually clear, bubbled angrily churning up dark mud. "When I'm gone," he answered softly, "that man over there will seek to do to Divei what others strive to do to the whole world. He is of those who leave no stone unturned to lose their own soul through ruining the lives of others."

As she continued to stare down aghast, "Leave it," he said, "it will calm down, now that he has passed. Some men are difficult, my joy. So are some women. Xenia the Prioress won't listen to me; she won't adopt the easier rule that my Lady herself has enjoined. She even opposes separating off the girls I choose, and wants others also to live at the mill, a mixed crowd. I've tried this way and that, to make it clear to her. Only the other day I told her I had noticed that women who've been married are determined folk, altogether too efficient. They can't be humble, poor, obedient, as my Lady wants these to be. Xenia wouldn't see it. Still, she's promised to let me have my way at the mill for the time being. You're abbess there, my joy."

"No, no."

"Yes. But you may continue in the old house, if you want to keep the old rule. You may. But your nuns, the miller girls, must not. They must live apart and their life must not be so rigorous. Solitude, for one thing, must not be allowed them. Whatever they do, wherever they go, let there always be at least two of them together. My Lady wishes it. She wants no rigours for these girls. Only obedience, prayer, and the deepest understanding of love.

Serafim's constant and detailed care of the new Foundation, to which he passed on most of the gifts brought to him by those who sought his direction, was the source of much grievance.

" Since a monk has no possessions, anything he is given belongs to his monastery, therefore Serafim gives to the mill that which belongs to us," John explained to the others.

A clever speaker, he won many to his point of view, " The miller girls," he said, " must be searched whenever they pass out through the gates with sacks. They're filching our property."

Three nuns were duly stopped, at different times, at different gates, and their sacks examined. But it so happened that these three carried nothing but stones and rubbish. " He has outwitted us," John concluded shrewdly, " but we know he does send to Divei stuffs and wine, rusks, candles, and oil. We know it. We've only got to persist, and we'll catch him out." But the monks refused to be made ridiculous in the eyes of the nuns, even if these eyes were downcast, and the lips never smiled only twitched, slightly, at the corners.

Then John took to passing several times a day, outside the hunchback's cell. Late one afternoon, hearing a fresh young laugh, he peeped in at the window. Serafim and a buxom wench stood close together speaking softly. There was no one else there, his hands rested on her shoulders. Her face, a pretty face, glowed with devotion as she stared at him with huge eyes, still brimming with tears, while her lips already parted with laughter. Slithering past, John went straight to the abbot.

Serafim was saying, " You must try and overcome, by

docile obedience, the wrath of this fairy-tale step-mother of yours, my joy. Just as in a fairy tale! And, when you marry, and have a home of your own, always remember that obedience must be met with love, love with obedience. Arrogance and pride can only lead to misery. Go in peace," he added, patting her on the cheek, "Look, they're bringing me a great sufferer; I promised to finish my morning's talk with him before they put him to bed."

Four men carefully lowered on to the floor a fifth, good looking, well built, but haggard and cramped with pain. "The more I think about our talk," Nicholas Motovilov said, "the less I understand how you could guess about this old, this constant yearning of mine to find out the true goal of man's life on earth. But tell me now, what is it, if it's neither prayer nor fasting nor any other things that priests insist on?"

"All that's very good," Serafim replied, "but it's no more than a means to an end. Our real goal is the re-acquiring of the Holy Spirit, that Adam lost for us. Every one can achieve this in his way and every way that leads to it is good, and the ways that lead there are infinitely varied because any action undertaken and carried out in the name of Christ can lead there. Even if it is a failure in other respects. Whereas a good action, no matter how good, undertaken in any other name may well be fruitful in some other way, but not in this."

They talked on in the quiet cell till late into the night. The four servants went off to get their supper. When they returned, the night was dark. The candles and sanctuary lamps, hardly perceptible before the ikons in sunlight, glowed like a sea of flame.

Next day they brought their sick master to the near hut where the cripple, surrounded by dense crowds, was busy lifting his last potatoes. The servants lowered their master to the ground, in a patch of sunlight, beside a tall pine.

"Father," Nicholas begged, as Serafim came towards him, " all physicians have given me up. I know that God alone can help me. But my prayers are not pure enough to rise to him. I've come to beg for yours."

" Do you believe ? " Serafim began his string of questions. " I do, I do," Nicholas answered with profound fervour, " would I be here if I didn't ? "

" Your faith has restored your health, then. You're well."

" How ' well,' when my men and you are supporting me on all sides."

" No, no. You're quite well. Every bit of you is completely whole. Let go," he addressed the men, " no further need of your help now." Then, taking hold of the sick man's shoulders, he raised him to his feet saying, " Stand firm. Take a firm stand on the ground. Have courage. Come on, you're all right." And beaming, " Isn't it grand, just look how well you can stand ! "

" Only because you're holding me," Nicholas protested.

Serafim let go, " Not at all. Come on, walk."

" I'll fall. When I do it hurts terribly, for days."

" You won't. The Lord has made you whole."

A stream of buoyancy surged through the sick man's released body, and, beside himself with joy, he advanced firmly, quickly.

" Stop," Serafim cautioned him, " enough. Remember you've three years of frightful illness behind you. Don't overdo it. Treasure your health, it's precious. Drive back to the guest house, and rest."

The crowd, too, hurried away, to spread the news. Serafim, his work finished, slowly walked home. Once again the leaves were turning and the forest stood in its brightest attire. The nights were growing cold, animals were getting ready to hibernate, birds were migrating south. In a narrow, winding path that led to a side gate, he met Nifont. The abbot looked disturbed, even distressed; when he spoke, the effort to overcome his embarrassment brought back into his voice and bearing a flicker of his old arrogance. "The monks are worried, dear Father. All these visits by women. We really think they should stop."

"Well, I can't go to Divei, you know, I'm not strong enough," Serafim answered with a simplicity that had become natural to him. "None of the older monks will promise to direct my girls after my death, let alone to go there now. And Father John, who is so anxious to, really isn't the right man. What shall we do?"

Nifont shifted his eyes uneasily from a sparrow chirping on a crimson branch, to a snail on the yellow sand; then looked up at a red squirrel hiding in the dark green overhead. "Well, yes," he mumbled, "the nuns too, of course. But we would be glad if you at least cut out these heart to heart talks with buxom young girls who think of nothing but marriage and finery, not of prayer and the austere life. You yourself have told others not to expose themselves unnecessarily to temptations of the flesh. Very real temptations, Father."

Serafim gazed down at the snail. Fat and slimy it turned its horns cautiously this way and that. Very softly he said, "I've looked into the face of God, Father."

"No doubt, no doubt," the abbot exclaimed, "I cast no slur on your achievements. Only they don't come in."

Serafim breathed, hardly above a whisper, "No flesh can see God. . . ." In the stillness that followed, a fir cone dropped beside the snail, branches swished overhead as the squirrel leapt higher, wings whirred as the sparrow flew away. Then all was perfectly still. ". . . And live," Nifont involuntarily finished the sentence.

"Father," Serafim begged kneeling in the sand. path and

touching the ground with his forehead, " for the good of Sarov that we both love, I beg of you, don't give heed to every scandal-monger that comes along. An abbot must have discrimination; above all else, he must have discrimination and a judgment of his own making."

" Get up, get up," Nifont fussed over him, " forget about it. We shall all forget about it."

" Why forget? I would have good come of it," Serafim sighed. But, once again, Nifont missed his meaning.

When winter came and there was no more work to do in his kitchen garden, Serafim resumed his felling. It was at this work that Nicholas, who had dedicated his restored life to Serafim and Divei, mostly found the cripple.

The snow, knee deep on the ground, was still falling thickly. " I've been thinking of prayer and the Church," Serafim said, seating Nicholas on a fresh stump and resting his own back against a felled pine. " It may well happen that a man wants to go to church but there's none near enough; when he wants to be charitable, there's no beggar about, or he himself has nothing to give; if he wishes earnestly to lead a pure life, circumstances and his own weakness may be against him. Longing to do this or that good deed, he may never find an opportunity for it. But prayer is always at hand for rich and poor, the great and the humble, the strong and the weak, the hale and the sick, the pure and the impure. This rising stream of supplication so easily brings down, as answer, the holy breath ! Then, once he's come, the Comforter, our prayer is a pure rejoicing. And where those who rejoice come together, there is the Church. And there the joy of each is no longer a fleck of golden dust. All dust, even gold dust, scatters before an adverse wind. But in the Church all the flecks of gold are fused into a mighty block that no storm can shatter, no downpour wash away. The block stands against all the wily or rabid onslaughts of the evil host." His voice dropped to a whisper, " As is known to those of whose joy it is made, the block is a golden ship, seaworthy as no other : its snow-white sails, woven by my Lady, are filled with the holy breath, the shining glory."

" If I could only see it once, that glory ! "

" Whenever we consciously do his will, we stand within it. We've grown blind to it, but it is there all right. Just as in the days when men said, 'we went and the Holy Ghost went with us,' 'we and the Holy Ghost decree.' "

" But how can I be certain of it, in these days ?"

Putting down his axe, Serafim came forward. Nicholas rose. The cripple gripped him by the shoulders and said, " We're both in the spirit now. Look at me."

" I can't. It hurts my eyes."

" Fear nothing. Look."

In the centre of a huge radiant sun, the well known, well loved faced smiled. Nicholas saw the speaking lips move, the expression in the deep blue eyes change. He heard the voice, felt the grip of hands. But these hands, as well as Nicholas's own shoulders and Serafim's body, were lost in a brightness that obliterated them and inundated the whole clearing, burnishing the flakes of falling snow and the snow on the ground to a glowing whiteness.

" How lovely," he sighed.

" In what way lovely ? "

" So quiet, such peace. In me and around me."

" What else ? "

" Such sweetness."

" What else ? "

" Such joy. My heart rings with it."

" What else ? "

" Warmth, a glowing warmth."

"What else?"

"A heavenly scent."

Reflecting the light, Serafim's eyes sparkled. "The grace of God is in you and you are in it. If you could only see how your face shines. Will you always remember the grace that has been lavished on you, my joy?"

"And me not even a monk!"

"That's nothing. It is to the man, not to his state or condition, that God says, 'Child, give me your heart.' If we give it, he comes."

A few days later, a distraught husband led into Serafim's cell, his pretty wife. Healthy until recently, she had fallen prey to the grim ailment popularly called "the fits."

Suddenly one afternoon, when walking with him in their garden, she shouted, "It spins, it spins, everything spins," and fell to the ground where, unconscious, she shook and trembled like a fish on the bank. As the fit began to abate, she gnashed her teeth and gnawed anything she could lay hands on. Only after she had fallen asleep, there in the path, was it possible to carry her into the house. A few days later she had a second fit. Then they grew more frequent and, for a year, she had one almost every day. The local physician sent her to one famous specialist after another, but all failed to restore her to health. The last one said, "Pray to God, my dear. Perhaps he can help you. I can't."

That night, Sandra saw in her sleep, an oldish woman, barefoot, lean of body but with a round face, come up to her and say, "Don't be afraid. I want to help you. Go to Serafim of Sarov, he knows how."

When Sandra woke, she told her dream to her mother who slept in her room. "Yes, yes. When you're a bit stronger, we'll go."

But again, the following night, Sandra saw the woman who said, "Why do you put it off? Serafim is waiting, he knows your sorrow, and wants to help."

Next day, husband, wife, and mother, set out for Sarov. When they entered Serafim's anteroom, it was crowded but the door of the cell was locked. The monk who had guided them through the winding passages, went up to the locked door and said aloud the habitual prayer. " Come on, Sandra, come on," Serafim exclaimed opening the door; and leading her into the cell and up to the ikon of Our Lady, " It's my Lady's work, her work of intercession. Thank her properly."

He gave the young woman some holy water to drink, and a bottle of it and three bits of dried bread to take home. " Take one little rusk a day, drinking a sip or two of the water with it. And go to Divei, find the tomb of the foundress, and thank her. It was she who called you. And, in future, whether I am alive or dead, whenever the anguish comes upon you, call me with all your heart. I'll hear you, and the anguish will go."

All barriers between the world of matter and the world of spirit were lifted now. He saw them playing into each other, interweaving and, sometimes, clashing. Often his anxiety was great. He saw the way of righting things, but had to leave it to men to follow his guidance or refuse it. Man's spirit is free, and must not be fettered or coerced.

One day, greatly perturbed, he sent for Helen. " My joy," he said, " my first serious charge you refused to accept fully."

" I'll accept any other," she broke in.

" I have another for you. Mika is very ill, over there, at Kuprianov's. Actually, the time has come for him to die. But I want him badly, to help the miller girls after I'm dead.

And he'll be left to us, to do this work, if another dies for him, as a charge, under obedience."

" Gladly, Father," she kissed his hand.

" Die then, my love," and he gave her his blessing to do so. As she crossed the threshold out of his cell, she fainted. Evpraxia, and others standing there, caught her in their arms, " What shall we do, there's nothing to put her on ? " " Put her in my coffin," Serafim said. He sprinkled her with holy water, then gave her some to drink. When she recovered, they drove her home to Divei. There she was put to bed, and died a few days later.

When Evpraxia, all in tears, came to Serafim, he exclaimed, " Again you weep, you silly joy ! If you had seen her soul rise like a dove and fly straight up to the Three in One. The cherubim and seraphim crossed their wings above her as she glided up. She too, is in attendance on my Lady now, praying constantly. And you weep ! "

But Evpraxia was not easily consoled. First Mary. Now Helen. She was very lonely. Though Serafim never spoke of her as the miller girls' abbess, he saw more of her than before, and confided much to her.

Tradition, using its conventional phraseology, colourfully describes the culmination of Serafim's confidence in Evpraxia : " Early in April, he told her to be sure and come again in two days time. When she arrived, he said, ' My Lady wants you to be here when she visits me this time. Kneel down.' Resting the Bible on her head, he read several passages out of it, then bidding her rise, said, ' Hold on to me firmly.' "

" Suddenly there came a sound as of the rushing of mighty wind through giant forests. Expectant silence followed. Then singing. Serafim knelt and raised his hands. Two angels, their golden hair reaching down to their shoulders, appeared holding in their hands flowering branches. They were followed by John the Baptist and

John the Divine, both clothed in shining white. Then came the Queen of Heaven with twelve maidens in attendance. Her scintillating cloak was of a colour which has no name in human language. Her dress was green as the spring shoots of larch ; on her head she wore a high crown. Her long, glossy hair hung loose about her back and shoulders. The girls around her in no way resembled each other but the beauty of each was perfect in its way. The cell was grown as spacious as the whole of heaven and earth. The air above it flickered as with the flames of a thousand candles. The light, though intense, was not disturbing. Evpraxia sank to the ground, overcome with awe. St. Mary touched her head with her hand, ' Get up, my girl,' she said. ' You've nothing to fear. Look, these girls of mine are very much like you. Go and speak to them.' She turned to Serafim, who stood beside John the Divine, ' Soon, my love, quite soon now, you'll be with us ; one of us, for ever.'

"The two Johns gave him their blessing, the girls kissed him on the cheek and, in a flash, the heavenly host were gone."

The decoding of the conventional language is not difficult : Serafim was granted the grace of introducing another person into the stream of untarrying mercy that had come to rest in him.

THE CONSUMMATE BIRTH

ASSAILED through many long years by storms and earthquakes, the place of rest, called Serafim, increasingly showed signs of erosion. In constant hard use, subject to time, it was falling to dust. But the man waxed more vigorous from month to month. " My flesh is dead," Serafim said to Paul, " but I am more alive than in my earliest childhood."

When he was not exclusively immersed in the joy of union with his creator, his interest still centred in the lives of those who sought him and clung to him. But his attention was slipping away from the visible to the secret pattern of their lives, and his feeling for the unity of all creation reached a new concreteness. At any time, in any place, he would detach himself from his surroundings and pray for a man in mortal danger, or a soul in danger of mortal sin. His mind found them at the right moment, the moment of their greatest need, no matter where they were.

Again, the tradition veils—or preserves for those who can raise the veil—the next achievement of the matured and mellowed friend of God : " One day, Serafim's door remained locked. In vain monks, nuns, and children intoned the prayer which, without saying it, begs for admittance. In the cell, Serafim wrestled. While at prayer, he got the intimation that one of the greatest sinners of the world lay dying. Sharpening his claws, a devil crouched by the deathbed, waiting to pounce on the soul and drag it down to his prince. Already, the dark host were busy preparing their feast of grim rejoicing. Imploring the Queen of Heaven's support, Serafim prayed to the Father in the name of the Son.

" In a remote country, on a bed of anguish surrounded by splendour, the dying man writhed and panted. In Serafim's small whitewashed cell, the old cripple's pure will kept his perfected mind fixed on the fate of the dying man's soul. Day passed into night, night into a new day ; and still the man of the lost soul writhed and panted, and Serafim, in great agony of soul but with undeflected purpose, prayed that this soul might be saved.

"At last he heard the Voice, ' The boon is granted. Serafim's compassion may flower in another's life. He may wash this soul and speed it home.'

"The fight with the brood of darkness lasted long, the cleansing of the soul was arduous work. Reeling with exhaustion Serafim could at last rest. He gazed with joyous love at the streak of light which, surrounded by a host of angels, sped up towards the golden gates. Craftily, the Prince of Pride emerged out of the abyss and, catching Serafim off his guard, crept up behind him. Frightfully wounded in the back, between the shoulder blades, in the one spot where the devil may directly attack human flesh, Serafim fell where he stood." The Mercy of God had long ago established itself in Serafim. Now he was permitted to deflect to himself the Wrath of God which other men attract through their lust for evil.

Early on the fourth day, Paul tried the door once again. It opened and he went in. From a sack of stones, on to which Serafim had dragged himself, he raised a haggard face, and smiled. " Father," gasped Paul bending down, " what happened ? "

" Nothing much."
" You're in pain ? "
" Yes."
" What can I do ? "
" Nothing."

He would have gladly returned to his former solitude, and entirely devoted the remaining days of his life to prayer : to the Godward prayer of praise and joy, and the manward prayer of intercession for the living, dying, and dead. But even more than prayer, the living demanded guidance. This, few of them were sensitive enough to receive otherwise than by word of mouth, and, while still alive, he could not bring himself to refuse them his word of counsel. But during the whole of that summer he spent his nights at the near hut, in prayer of perfect union, and returned to his cell only after sunrise; sometimes long after sunrise.

All day, wherever they found him, they clustered round. Unable to speak to all, he singled out the very young and the very old. " The middle of man's life, when his worldly passions have full sway, matters least," he told Evpraxia. " At that time he must only learn indifference to his own happiness and unhappiness, to success and failure : so that he may step out of all these tribulations, overshadowed by the still wings of muted joy. But in the beginning and towards the end of a life, every trifle is of the greatest importance."

Sometimes he would address the crowd, " Men cannot be too gentle, too kind. Shun even to appear harsh in your treatment of each other. But remember, no work of kindness or charity can bring down to earth the holy breath, unless it is done in the name of Christ. When it is, joy, radiant joy, streams from the face of him who gives and kindles joy in the heart of him who receives. All condemnation is of the devil. Never condemn each other. Not even those whom you catch at the evil deed. We condemn others only because we shun knowing ourselves. When we gaze at our own failings, we see such a morass of filth, that nothing in another can equal it. That is why we turn away, and make much of the faults of others. Keep away from the spilling of speech. Instead of condemning others, strive to reach the inner peace. Keep silent, refrain from judgment. This will raise you above the deadly arrows of slander, insult, outrage, and will shield your glowing hearts against the evil that creeps around."

Dressed in white, with white wisps of hair gleaming round his pink face, with dark blue eyes radiating a vitality generated by his keen spirit, Serafim stood against the green background on a clearing dappled with sunlight and shadow—like the soul of a transfigured world, the spirit of a forest once dark but now luminous and joyful.

Joy was in his nature. Now, through incessant effort, its enriched stream overflowed to all, reviving them. A life-giving stream, it washed away despondency and sorrow.

Sometimes younger monks who were going through their time of hopelessness, hardest to bear in the poignant melancholy of autumn, turned to him. A novice overcome by wretchedness, begged an almost equally dejected young monk to join him in his walk, after evensong. They left the compound and, softly talking of their own sadness, the sorrows of the world, and the essence of despair, slowly strolled round the monastery walls. Passing by the stable yard, they came to the path that led to the Well.

"Let's turn off," said the novice, "with this worm gnawing at my heart I couldn't bear to meet Serafim."

But he had already joined them; his white habit, pulled up in front and behind, bulged funnily at the waist: he had stuffed it into his belt as he did when at work. At the sides, it hung low. A very large, bright green shawl, flung about him, fluttered in the wind. One end was caught round his neck and tied there; another trailed on the ground behind. His eyes flashed, his step was almost that of a dance. With outstretched arms he came close up to the young men and gave them his blessing. He sang, "Fill my heart with joy, St. Mary, conqueror of the sin of sorrow, vessel gladly bearing joy." Then taking hold of their hands he called out, "Away with despondency. There is nothing Christ has not conquered. Nothing."

At his approach, their mood had calmed, and mirrored his. Their anguish was gone, and they smiled. Singing, he continued on his way, his thin white hair blowing in the cold wind. Dry leaves, caught in the fringes of the long green shawl, scraped the sand path behind him. The young men sighed, comforted. Returning, each to his cell, they prepared for a long night of vigil and of prayer.

When a woman's time is come, no efforts of hers or of those round her can stop the birth of the child. Whatever the reasons for putting it off, this cannot be done; not even for an hour. It is the same with death.

Serafim was slipping away. Not even his compassion, true and determined as it was, could retain him. As time advanced, his attention to men was increasingly towards the heavenly, secret, significance of their lives. He would often avoid his visitors when most engrossed in them, and hide like a child behind trees and bushes, or jump out of his window and run away.

Alone among the snow-powdered giants, that stood stark and bare hibernating in their own way, he passed into the golden city; and implored the heavenly host to help the men for whom he was concerned; to help every one toward the right unravelling of his skein of life.

Serafim hobbled back to the monastery, with his heart torn and yet comforted, only to be at once surrounded by some of those he had prayed for. His eyes too full of light, his ears too full of song, he could no longer teach, but silently spread his joy to them, whispering, " The Lord is arisen; arisen." Or gave them his blessing murmuring, " Love joins love; devotion meets obedience; then comes freedom; the true freedom."

At night, he could no longer sleep resting on his sacks of stones. If at all, he slept crouching in his anteroom, by his coffin, resting his arms on its edge, his head on his arms. The wound in his back caused him constant pain.

A man among men, he already lived the full life of the blessed: the two-fold life where the prayer of praise is joy, the prayer of intercession is suffering. When they are perfectly balanced, they keep the blessed within the fold of human kind. For in no other kingdom are joy and suffering so perfectly balanced as in the kingdom of man. These two basic human conditions, heightened to the intensity attained in blessedness, and balanced as they can be only on the highest rung of the scale, were become the fabric of his life. His cell was a corner of heaven come down to earth.

One evening Paul came into the anteroom in search of a light. Serafim was standing by his coffin, deep in thought. He looked up, and together they went into the cell.

"With the breath of thy Comforter make me warm, O Lord," Serafim whispered.

"Oh, I thought I saw no light in that sanctuary lamp a moment ago," Paul exclaimed, "but now, it's blazing brighter than the rest!" "Light your candle from it," said Serafim; then added, "Alexander Bezobrazov will be coming soon. But I shan't see him. Tell him I am sorry."

Blowing out the candle which Paul held, he mused, "So will my life be extinguished; and your carnal eyes will see me no more." "Father," whispered Paul beseechingly. "Don't sorrow, my joy," Serafim smiled, "it is gladness, gladness." Paul had never seen the cripple so radiant, nor himself had felt so much at peace.

On Christmas day, after mass, Serafim spoke to Nifont: He asked to be buried near the altar of the Cathedral of the Dormition, on a spot where, soon after he came out of enclosure, he had put a large boulder, brought up from below the hill.

New Year's day fell on a Sunday. After mass, he went

the round of all the monks, kissing them on the cheek and saying, " A day of coronals and wreaths. Lift your hearts. Keep them warm."

Back in his cell, he saw a few visitors. Among others, Evpraxia to whom he gave two hundred rubles. " Tell Mother Xenia to buy grain with it. Needy times ahead." And as she sighed wearily and sadly, " You're not going to weep again ! My Lady herself is your director now." Evpraxia brushed away a tear. " All of you girls," he said earnestly, " must come to my grave whenever sorrow weighs you down. Kneeling there, tell me all about it. I'll hear you, and your sorrow will be lifted. As I've lived with you of late, so I will continue to live. Partaking of the joy and suffering of the blessed, I will remain attentive to your sorrows. To all sorrow. Till the day of the Last Judgment."

Three times Paul saw him leave his cell, and go to the place where he was to be buried. He stood there long, looking down at the snow, or into the ground beneath it. In the evening Paul heard him sing the Easter hymns of resurrection.

Next morning early, hurrying to mass, Paul noticed a strong smell of smoke in the anteroom. Receiving no answer to the prayer he intoned before Serafim's locked door, he went out into the porch and called to the passing monks and novices, " There's a strong smell of smoke here, can you feel it ? Serafim must have gone to the hut again, and left his candles burning ! "

The novice, whom Serafim had comforted, rushed in and wrenched the door from its hinges. Next to the threshhold a heap of sacks lay smouldering : a candle, never before placed there, had fallen on to them.

Pale dawn glimmered in the east. The cell was silent, dark, full of thick smoke. Some of the men threw snow on the sacks, others brought light.

Serafim, arms crossed on his chest, knelt before the ikon of Our Lady of Tenderness. His eyes were closed. " Asleep. Grown weary in his night-long vigil. So old ! " said the novice in a hushed voice.

Taking the kneeling figure by the shoulders, Paul gently shook it. Through the thin linen habit, the dead flesh felt cold. Agatha's cross glinted in the candle light.

It was, according to the Julian Calendar, the second of January, 1833. A week later, in the small town of Kursk, Alexis Moshnin—retired merchant-builder—died peacefully, surrounded by his large family. He was seventy-eight years old.

More than a hundred years had passed since the birth of Prokhor Moshnin. On 1 August, 1903, Serafim of Sarov was canonized. The sun—the fierce Russian sun that for centuries had caused the peasant to pit his prayers against the fiery breath of the drought—blazed down on an endless, thickly packed procession which, headed by church dignitaries, the Tsar, the Tsarina, the Tsar's mother and five other members of the Imperial Family, slowly made its way to the humble grave by the Old Church.

All sang. Those who did not carry church banners or ikons held lighted candles. The vestments, made of cloth of gold embroidered with six-winged seraphs, were a gift of the Monarch. He, his uncles, and his retinue, all wore the white summer tunic of the Russian army. The sun glinted off stiff epaulets, brass buttons, vestments, ikons, gold and enamelled crucifixes.

The forest of Temniki hummed with great crowds that gathered there in the last fortnight, coming from all over Russia by road, railway, and waterway. Many had come on foot taking weeks, or even months, to get there. The old, solidly built guest houses, and the log huts hurriedly put up for the occasion, were crammed ; the monastery grounds and churches were congested; the heat was suffocating.

Before the procession poured out of the Cathedral, the Metropolitan explained that they were about to sing the last Requiem for the humble monk Serafim. Thereafter St. Serafim would be prayed to, not prayed for.* Thereafter Russians would beseech him to intercede for sinners, to succour the sorely smitten.

Later that day, the relics were placed in a sumptuous Baroque shrine. The sanctuary lamps, hung from ropes of priceless pearls, shone like a forest of stalactites in an Arabian tale; set with precious stones, they were the handiwork of the best jewellers of the country.

Soon the crowds of pilgrims thinned, trickled away, dispersed. Many had heard of Serafim for the first time when his canonization was mooted and discussed; returning to their homes and occupations, they retained a clearer impression of the pomp and of the splendour than of him who had caused the display: the cripple, whose life was stripped even of the most essential necessaries.

But when the Japanese War called the Russian armies east, and the revolution of 1905 shook the country, the intercessor was remembered by wives and mothers. In the following decade—one of hectic eagerness for money, advancement, and worldly success—he was often entreated to guard ambitious men and women against the dangers they ran and the temptations they sought.

Though vivid, the "plutocratic period" of Russian history was short-lived. The "Russian *tiers-état*," looking forward to the time when they would lead their country, supported the revolutionaries against Tsar and gentry. But in 1914 they heard their death knell. When, in 1917, the butchery on the Western fronts of Russia was called off,

* The Metropolitan Antony must have had in mind only the special services, for during the celebration of the Eucharist—when all are prayed for—saints, prophets, and even angels are included.

butchery did not cease; swiftly it spread over the whole country in a gigantic civil war.

By this time Serafim, the man of prayer, had become to the Christians of Russia the saint beloved above all others; a quiet light, steadily shining in the midst of whirling darkness. Men, women, and particularly the young, torn between conflicting allegiances, turned to him for guidance, for a new serenity and inner poise, for strength of mind and soul; desiring to draw nearer to their saint, they sought to learn more about him. Surmises as well as facts were discussed, compared, and eventually incorporated into the legend which had begun to take form before Serafim's death.

At the time of the canonization, relevant facts deemed to be appropriate had been fixed in official Lives; during the civil war strands of the floating legend were gathered in the district sanctified by the endeavours of Serafim the cripple, and the achievements of Serafim the saint. In the late twenties, the Temniki became a vast lumber camp; in the dark forest of old pines, communities came to live very different from the one Serafim had joined.

Life's jungle, always rich in weeds, has shaped according to its law. Man, apt to outdo the jungle in weeds, excels in felling the straightest trees—the first to be condemned. But in the commercially exploited forest of Temniki, where the churches have been destroyed and the monastery buildings are put to other uses, a light still hovers over the hill, the air above still rings with peals of many bells; if you have eyes to see, and ears to hear. The soil of the forest holds its dead gently, and reverently drinks the blood of its wounded; the beasts of the forest do not unearth the dead; birds sing litanies over the graves. For men may come and change and go, but the creatures of this forest abidingly treasure their hard won tradition: their reverence for God's unhappiest creature, man. The trees of Temniki, earth's arms stretched skyward because of her joy in the nearness of heaven, still rise exultantly and, as the wind blows through them, whisper, lest men should forget:

Holy Father Serafim, pray to the Lord our God for our salvation!

NOTE ON BIOGRAPHICAL DATA

SOME dates of Serafim's childhood cannot be fixed because the year of his birth, usually assumed to be 1759, is uncertain though the day, 19 July O.S., is undisputed. The *Russian Encyclopædia* usually known as " Brockhaus and Ephron " (St. Petersburg 1900) places it in 1760, N. Levitski (Moscow 1905) in 1754, Dr. Zernov (London 1937) in 1750. Levitski tried to ascertain some dates concerning Serafim's family, the Moshnins of Kursk. He failed to find the entry of Prokhor's christening in the local church registers, but discovered one of his " confession " in 1768, where his age is given as 14. Still, there is no reason to treat this as conclusive evidence : the child of a devout family would be going to confession from the age of seven, and the entries of age, and even of Christian names, were often careless. The question must remain open, but oral tradition has preserved (or added) details which suggest 1759 as the date of Prokhor's birth.

There are other discrepancies. Prokhor at his father's death was, according to the tradition, a few months old : in most *Lives* he is mentioned vaguely as being a small child ; the Archimandrite Sergius (Moscow 1858) who knew Serafim personally, and an anonymous author (Moscow 1883) give his age as three. Levitski, in his perusal of the registers found that " the merchant Isidor, son of Ivan, Moshnin died on 10 May, 1760 aged 43." This would make Prokhor, if born in 1759, a little over nine and a half months at his father's death. But if he was then three, the year of his birth must be 1756 or 1755, neither of which was ever suggested; and if born in 1760, as stated in the *Encyclopædia* he would have been a posthumous child, a fact which could hardly have escaped notice but is nowhere mentioned.

Serafim's mother is usually described as young, or even very young, at the time of her husband's death. But Levitski found the entry of her death under date of 28 Feb. 1800: "Widowed townswoman Agatha, daughter of Photius, wife of Isidor Moshnin, aged 72." This would make her 27 at the birth of her first child, Alexis, and 31 at Prokhor's; a middle-aged woman according to Russian ideas, if this entry is correct.

Prokhor's fall from the belfry is uniformly stated as having occurred when he was seven; his illness, cured by the ikon, when he was ten. The year of his arrival at Sarov is accepted as 1778 or 1779; but here again the day—the eve of the feast of the dedication of Our Lady—is unquestioned. The legend does not mention the year but gives his age as nineteen.

There is no disagreement about most dates of Serafim's life at Sarov, but the duration of his first attack of dropsy is uncertain. Most biographers say that he fell ill in 1780, was bed-ridden for three years, then visited Kursk and saw his mother shortly before her death; others—while keeping to the gist of the story—that he was cured in 1780. According to Professor Tsarev (Kazan 1903) the illness was long, but he does not specify how long. The floating tradition says Serafim was ill about one year.

Thus there is not much conclusive evidence about the early dates of Serafim's life, whether provided by biographers or registers. The tradition is sometimes closer to the registers than the official biographies, but while it is a true mirror of popular preferences, and subtly reveals the people's attitude to life, it cannot be taken to refute or corroborate particular facts. The matter of Agatha's age can serve as example. Russians incline to find special virtue in the fortitude of the weak and the immature who require " grace " to overcome physical handicaps and lack of experience: the floating tradition presents Agatha as very young and of delicate health when she takes over the business. Still, differences between the various accounts concern mere details. The trend and general pattern of Serafim's life are the same in written record and popular tradition, although a different set of points is singled out, stressed and elaborated. On the whole, the written record gives precedence to miracles and virtues, whereas the tradition prefers psychological detail and dramatic situations. Two interpretations of the ban on women's visits to Serafim's Far Hut are an apposite example.

Most biographers say that Serafim himself, distressed by the unseemliness of women's visits, begged the abbot to put a stop to them; the abbot, engrossed in other business, waived the plea as unworthy of his attention; thereupon Serafim asked only for the abbot's blessing of the virtuous decision which Our Lady had promised to implement; the blessing given, Our Lady " deflected " the women, and the saint lived on, serene, and with his reputation untarnished. The event, so tidily described, is treated in a very different manner by the tradition where the initiative is attributed to hostile monks whose interference almost breaks Serafim's heart.

Of Prokhor's childhood, only the miracles are mentioned in the official biographies; the legend fills his early years with intimate detail, and into his years in the monastery it weaves the common people's traditional knowledge of the contemplative way. The " tellers " of the legend, the *skazateli*, not satisfied with the biographers' reticence on all except the saint's scale of achievements, try to explain how the achievements were attained and at what cost.

It is partly the desire better to understand Serafim's personality and the nature of his ascent, that has led the *skazateli* to dwell on secondary characters dismissed in the official *Lives* with a superficial pious phrase or two. And it has led them to create three characters: Prokhor's "Auntie," his tutor Lukich, and Galeena a cousin of his sister-in-law. Grisha the Fool is a remarkable figure in the popular tradition; his preoccupation with the Old Believers suggests that this group of dissenters has had a hand in shaping him. But the biographers only mention him as a *iurodivyi* who prophesied to Prokhor's mother about her infant son, and later had considerable influence on the growing boy.

Prokhor's desire to be an architect and to go abroad cannot be traced in the written record, but is elaborated by the legend. And when a concentration camp for defaulting foreign communists was set up in the Temniki, the saying went round that Serafim had chosen the better portion in not going abroad to help unbelievers in his lifetime: things had worked out for the best in the end— now, at their time of greatest sorrow and when he himself dwells very near to God, he draws foreign unbelievers to his forest and serves them better than he could have done in their own country in his youth. Bezobrazov's talk with Serafim about the Jews is also unrecorded. I heard it twice: from an old local peasant, and from a recidivist thief—an unbeliever—the son of a Jew by a Circasian woman.

The legend-tellers show preoccupation with the hermit's attitude to the Eucharist. In a sense, the Orthodox position on Communion is definite: an ordained celebrant and a consecrated altar—or to be exact the *antimins*—are required, and every member of the Church is expected to communicate at least once a year; laxity or indifference are tantamount to wilful severance from the body of the faithful— a " falling into heresy." And yet, since the days of the Desert Fathers many saintly hermits have gone without, for years. Not that they spurned or did not desire it, but the physical and social conditions which made frequent, or even yearly, communion impossible for them were accepted as insuperable, apparently without agitation or demur. It would seem that frequent Communion and the solitary life are easily regarded as incompatible in the East, and that a certain tension between them is thought unavoidable : the Orthodox Mass, celebrated with dignity and splendour, is celebrated by the priest for the flock ; but dignity, splendour, and the presence of men clash with the silent hermit's life in cave, wattle hut, or rude log cabin. And so, " Which of two actions, both right yet incompatible, should be preferred ? " asks the Russian who, whether educated or not, delights in wrestling with riddles of this nature. In the legend of Serafim the tension is used to show obedience to the Church as more important than either—an attitude not entirely unlike St. Teresa's, in her harsh condemnation of the nuns who struck and threatened to die when deprived of the Eucharist through circumstances beyond their superior's control.

After much consideration I have thought best to introduce some imaginary detail into the English version of this Russian legend, chiefly around Lukich and Prokhor's aunt. The floating tradition, created by Russians for Russians, cleverly uses mere indications—antiquated or clipped words and phrases, and barbarisms—to evoke a cluster of overtones that make its characters live. If, however, they are to come to life for a foreign public, a different idiom occasionally has to be adopted : explicit detail must replace subtle indications ; and wherever greater clarity seemed necessary, I have substituted the cruder idiom for the more elusive. Landscape and the historical setting are introduced with a similar end in view.

Some points in Serafim's later life are incorrectly rendered by the popular tradition : the " child Mary " was apparently a sister of the nun Paraskeva, not of a " woman unhappily married " ; and according to Motovilov's report—which there is no reason to question—he had only one important talk with Serafim, in the forest in winter; the popular tradition makes two talks of it, and transfers one into the cell before Motovilov is cured of his sickness. Much of the conversation is omitted by the *skazateli*, while its points of general appeal are embellished.

Where biographers and *skazateli* differ, I have kept to the floating tradition; those passages where the official records almost verbally follow the narrative of the floating tradition, I have placed in quotes. But my concern has been with the legend, not the *Lives*.